M

Alexander, Gary,
1941-

Pigeon blood

$16.95

DATE DUE		
APR 21 2004		
FEB 15 2005		

PIGEON BLOOD

PIGEON BLOOD

Gary Alexander

Walker and Company
New York

M

3 -88 BT 1700

Copyright © 1988 by Gary Alexander

First published in the United States of America in 1988 by the Walker Publishing Company, Inc.

Published simultaneously in Canada by Thomas Allen & Son Canada, Limited, Markham, Ontario.

Printed in the United States of America

Library of Congress Cataloging-in-Publication Data

Alexander, Gary, 1941–
  Pigeon blood.

  I. Title.
PS3551.L3554P54   1988   813'.54   87-23025
ISBN 0-8027-5700-6

10 9 8 7 6 5 4 3 2 1

The author apologizes to the Socialist Republic of the Union of Burma, the People's Republic of China, the Lao People's Democratic Republic, and the Kingdom of Thailand for geographic distortions and for encroachment of their borders. Tolerance is also appreciated for liberties taken with the topography and climate of the region.

THE KINGDOM OF LUONG

PROLOGUE

NATIONS ARE CREATED by accident or by force. The Kingdom of Luong was not. It does not exist. It is as fictional as the following events and characters, but for purposes of this story, we can presume that Luong . . .

. . . is a constitutional monarchy often referred to as the fourth Indochina protectorate.

. . . became a French colony in 1889 and was granted independence in 1954.

. . . is roughly the size and shape of Louisiana, though the toe of the boot points up, northward, nudging China. The sole and heel border Laos and Thailand. Burma surrounds the upper.

. . . is a landlocked backwater of one and a half million people. Hickorn, the capital, has a population of two hundred thousand and is in the lowlands, abutting the Ma San River. Obon, the only other city of note, has fifty thousand inhabitants and is located in the northern highlands.

. . . is mountainous in the highlands, lush and torrid in the southern river valleys.

. . . is a nominal exporter of rice, tobacco, tin, and hardwood timber. Opium gum grown in the highlands is the only cash crop of substance.

. . . is self-sufficient in agriculture. Both the ability to feed itself and the political apathy of the populace allowed the Kingdom of Luong to avoid the strife suffered by Laos, Cambodia, and Vietnam. Neighboring Marxist insurgents have had their own problems, and even the most hawkish Pentagon analysts remain unable to project the Luongan domino falling against anything. The communist Luong Rouge movement, impoverished and ignored, is relegated to the status of nuisance.

. . . is ruled by seventy-six-year-old Prince Novisad Pakse, a consummate neutralist whose abiding passion is pocket billiards.

. . . has as its Hickorn Superintendent of Police a man named Bamsan Kiet, a man who intensely dislikes being awakened from a sound sleep.

PIGEON BLOOD

TO ROYAL LUONGAN
MILITARY ACADEMY (6 KM)

FOH TEN
(DRAGON'S BILE)

FOH TEN BRIDGE

NATIONAL
STADIUM

SAVHANA
ISLAND

DOCKS

NEVER ACCURATELY
MAPPED

FERRY

MA SAN RIVER

MA SAN BOULEVARD

RICHARD NIXON BOULEVARD

TO HICKORN
INTERNATIONAL
AIRPORT (4 KM)

PARK

11

AVENUE CHÉ GUEVARA

MU HICKORN

9

2

AVENUE DWIGHT EISENHOWER

4

MU SAVHANA

AVENUE IRVING CRANE

PARK

1

10   AVENUE MAO TSE-TUNG*

RUE WILLIE MOSCONI

AVENUE JOHN F. KENNEDY

7

PARK

PARK

AVENUE LEONID BREZHNEV

PARK

5

3

MU LUONG

RUE HO CHI MINH

MU PAKSE

AVENUE ALEXANDRE LOUBET

RUE POL POT

6

RUE NE WIN

PARK

*

AVENUE CHARLES DE GAULLE

8

TO LUONG
UNIVERSITY

N
W — E
S

DOWNTOWN
HICKORN

*TO BE AVENUE RONALD REAGAN   "PASSAGE LUTHER LASSI"

1. NATIONAL BANK
2. NATIONAL ASSEMBLY
3. ROYAL PALACE AND GROUNDS
4. UNITED STATES EMBASSY
5. STATUE OF PRINCE SAVHANA
6. SOVIET EMBASSY

7. HICKORN CONTINENTAL
8. SUSAN'S APARTMENT
9. CATHEDRAL
10. LOCATION OF
    STREET-RENAMING CER
11. KIET'S VILLA

1

"SIR, THERE HAS been a murder."

Superintendent Bamsan Kiet blinked. Captain Binh's flashlight resembled a monstrous firefly. Kiet swatted it away from his face.

"A murder?" he muttered.

"Superintendent, every door in your villa is unlocked. I walked right in. I could have been a burglar!"

One year in America and the young captain confuses Hickorn with New York City. How many times since his return has he lectured me on residential security? Kiet wondered. How often has he regaled me with stories of dope fiends clawing through barred windows to steal silverware and videotape recorders to finance their habits?

"A murder?" Kiet muttered again, more awake.

"Yes, sir. Will you come with me to the scene?"

Such enthusiasm, Kiet thought. Since his internship with the District of Columbia police, Binh had ached to test his knowledge on a bona fide homicide.

"Binh," he said, closing his eyes, "Of course there has been a murder. It is already October and only three people have been killed in Hickorn this year. All were unfaithful wives sent on a cruise across the River Styx by their husbands. We were overdue for another. Do your investigation, arrest the poor wretch, and report to me in the morning."

1

"It is the morning, Superintendent. Nearly seven o'clock."

"Morning is a matter of interpretation," Kiet said, yawning.

"Superintendent, the victim is a foreigner."

Kiet groaned, sat up, and began to put on his trousers. He was a heavy man, wide and tall, a rarity among his small, lithe countrymen. In his younger days, he had been described as Buddha-like by admiring young ladies, but the bulk he now carried was a burden, no longer attractive on a middle-aged widower.

"What breed of foreigner?"

"An American."

Kiet groaned again. When a Luongan died violently, it was usually a case of love flaring into hatred, a crime easily solved. But with foreigners, especially Americans and Russians, the motive was likely to be politics or business. Which always meant complexities and headaches.

"What happened? Who was the victim?"

"At the airport, in the pilot's seat of his airplane."

"Splendid. You have answered *where*."

"Oh, we are not exactly sure what happened. The dead man is Denny McCloud. He ran a charter and freight service called Luong Express. Airport employees found him an hour ago."

"Better you show me." Kiet said, rising unsteadily. "If you must."

2

2

HICKORN INTERNATIONAL AIRPORT'S terminal was a tiered stucco affair of a style once categorized by a Canadian travel writer as French Colonial Chintz. The facility was four kilometers north of downtown, on Richard Nixon Boulevard. Lettering on the boulevard side proclaimed H CKO N. Vegetation flourished in runway cracks. Despite this gentle shabbiness, Hickorn International was truly international. The Ma San River, respectably wide at Hickorn's docks, expended itself in malarial tributaries ten kilometers from the Thai border. The only way out of Luong, except for footpaths through mountain passes and double-canopy jungle, was up.

Binh and Kiet drove past the terminal onto an apron leading to aircraft hangars. Their destination was a twin-engine plane parked on the macadam and the dozen or so Hickorn policemen and airport security officers milling about it. The plane was painted a dull silver, LUONG EXPRESS crudely stenciled on its fuselage.

"I expect a remarkable challenge on this case," Binh said. "Police science is a skill that must be constantly sharpened, don't you agree?"

Kiet did not reply. It was much too early in the day for Binh's zeal. While Kiet was hastily dressed in trousers, sandals, and yesterday's shirt, his young adjutant was resplendent in a starched white uniform, gold captain's pips gleaming on shoulder boards. Even his appearance was exhausting.

"Evidently McCloud was preparing to take off last night," Binh continued. "Security personnel grew suspicious when the airplane didn't move. They discovered him just before dawn. He had been repeatedly stabbed."

"Eight or ten hours were required to arouse their curiosity? And why is Luong Express unfamiliar to me?"

"It's a small operation, as I understand. Just McCloud and the plane, which I'm told is a de Havilland Caribou. McCloud flew chartered freight and passengers between Obon and Hickorn. About twice a week he went to Bangkok. I checked our files at Headquarters. McCloud has never been arrested by us. A computer, by the way, would make that job much simpler, Superintendent, and if I could—what?"

Binh slammed on the brakes, jumped out of the old Citroën, and began screaming at two Hickorn uniforms who were placing the blanketed corpse of Denny McCloud on a stretcher. "You idiots! You shouldn't have moved him. You're ruining evidence."

Kiet got out of the car slowly, catching a disagreeable whiff of scorched brake lining. There was no money in his departmental budget for replacement of brake linings; he would have to discuss this element of police science with Binh. But later.

Nor did he now interrupt Binh's tirade by reminding him that not much evidence could be ruined by moving a body that had been putrefying in tropical heat for many hours. Such a reminder would accomplish nothing but humiliation, a devastating loss of face in the company of Binh's subordinates. More important, the unthinking policeman had spared Kiet the ordeal of viewing the late Denny McCloud. Luong's ranking civilian law enforcement officer fell violently ill at the sight of human carnage. This was Bamsan Kiet's deepest secret.

After Binh had properly cowed the pair, Kiet suggested that they go aboard the Caribou. The airplane was

4

obviously old, its silver paint flecked in spots, revealing an olive drab undercoat. Oil streaked both engine nacelles. Tire tread on the landing gear was a memory.

The interior was spartan—canvas seats and a roller track in the aisle for cargo. The path to the cockpit narrowed under the wings, partially blocked by fuel tanks riveted to bulkheads. The metalwork, though crude, was shiny and new.

Kiet noticed that everything that could be considered a nook or cranny, including the instrument panel and access covers, had been pried open or off. Two suitcases and a duffle bag were slashed and torn into pieces, clothing and toilet articles scattered every which way. Blood smeared the pilot and copilot seats, the control yoke, the windows, everything. Kiet visualized the struggle. He took a deep breath and backpedaled from the cockpit.

"Whoever did this was looking for something," Binh observed. "Something small. But did they find it?"

"What concerns me more is the time they had to accomplish this—this slaughter."

The Hickorn International Airport manager, Lon Min, a natty little man who favored cotton jumpsuits imported from Paris, was waiting outside the plane. Lon Min was married to a second cousin of Prince Pakse and also held the title of Associate Deputy Minister of Transportation.

Kiet had no quarrel with nepotism per se. Family gossip in the bureaucracy had squashed several coup d'etat plots against His Royal Highness before the eggs hatched, but sometimes it went too far. Kiet regarded Lon Min as prissy and corrupt. If it could be proven that Min's hands were sunken to the elbows in opium smuggling, Kiet would not faint from shock.

"Superintendent, this is a tragedy and a black mark on me," Min said. "I am at your disposal."

"Thank you. Tell me what you can."

"McCloud landed from Obon about five P.M., " said Lon Min. "He had brought in soldiers. Some were on furlough, some were here to be awarded medals for that skirmish last week where so many Rouge guerrillas were killed."

Kiet was surprised. "Denny McCloud flew troops?"

"Yes. He had a government contract. Whenever military aircraft were unavailable, McCloud handled the overflow. The army was his largest client."

Kiet's next thought was, Who did McCloud pay for his contract, who did he pay to insure that government aircraft were regularly "unavailable"?

"Then after five o'clock?"

"He filed a flight plan to Bangkok, an eight P.M. departure. McCloud wanted to leave earlier. He was an impatient sort, like most Westerners are. Arranging for refueling and refueling itself takes time, you know. Westerners do not understand the Luongan pace."

"McCloud's plane has extra gasoline tanks?"

"Yes. Auxiliary tanks were installed two weeks ago. It extended his range considerably."

"If McCloud's business took him farther than Bangkok, which is only seven hundred kilometers from Hickorn, why did he need extra tanks?

"I don't know, Superintendent. He didn't confide in me, but I can inquire."

"Please don't trouble yourself with my responsibilities. What was McCloud's mission to Bangkok?"

"According to his flight plan, he was shipping a thousand kilograms of rice."

"A long ton of rice? Really? I did not see a single sack, a single grain of rice. Did you, Captain?"

Binh shook his head.

"I was off duty," Min said stiffly. "I would have detected the irregularity. I am going to fine some of my underlings and demote my night customs supervisor."

6

"An invisible thousand kilos of rice. Do you have a manifest and passenger list of McCloud's Obon-to-Hickorn flight?"

"That is strangely missing. A procedural omission, I fear."

"Yet another irregularity," Kiet said sourly. "How is it that the Caribou was parked all night without being noticed? The ruckus inside it must have been loud and fierce."

"There is no evening shift of mechanics at the hangars, and if you will look, Superintendent, you will see that the hangars obscure any view from the terminal."

Kiet pointed at the control tower. A silhouette sat motionless inside four walls of tinted glass. Snoozing? Air traffic at Hickorn International was not dense.

"I have already spoken to my night tower operator. He regrets being unable to help. This area is not strongly lighted, you know."

Min's hands were on his hips, his tone increasingly shrill—a combination of fear and arrogance. Kiet knew that in a moment Min would remind him of his ministry post and of his connection to the royal family, and refuse further cooperation. The peacock was too frightened and too stupid to realize that his influence was marginal. Kiet decided to ease off. This session was lost anyway, and a relaxed Lon Min might be of use another time.

"You are right, of course. I apologize if I sound harsh. Murder investigations do that to me," Kiet said. "Did you know Mr. McCloud?"

"We were acquaintances, not friends," Min said, speaking more easily. "He was loud and demanding, as Caucasians tend to be, a man as tall and husky as yourself, Superintendent. He had a hearty laugh and liked to slap people on the back. His face and hair were red. The hair was thinning and it amused me how he combed it from where it grew to where it didn't. He was

afflicted with that Caucasian skin disease they call freck-
les. He spent money freely and had a reputation as a
womanizer. He lived in a room at the Hickorn Continental. He paid his tie-down fees and his fuel bills promptly.
Beyond that, he was a stranger. If he planned to leave
Luong for good, he didn't inform me."

Kiet thanked Min and shook his hand. When Min was
gone, Kiet conferred with Binh.

"Opium, Superintendent?"

"Likely." Royal Luongan Army soldiers stationed in
the highlands claimed to combat the Luong Rouge and
the opium bandits. In reality they did neither. The lower
ranks supplemented their meager pay on scraps of the
drug trade and senior officers grew wealthy. Because
illegal opium was Luong's primary source of hard currency, too many condoned the practice.

Opium had never earned Kiet a single dollar or franc
or yen or Luongan zin. If any of his officers were caught
participating in the business, they were dismissed from
the force and prosecuted. Still, he did not pursue the
dealers as he knew he should. An unspoken mandate
from those in power held him in leash unless there was
outside political pressure—a periodic "drive" or "campaign" by United States narcotics authorities, for instance. The rationalization that heroin poisoning of Chicago and Philadelphia children was not a Luongan
problem didn't satisfy him. It disrupted his sleep, it made
him feel weak and effeminate. In a murder investigation,
however, if opium was going to be mixed in with homicide, there would be no protection for the criminals.
Kiet's mood improved slightly.

"In America, if you cheat somebody on a narcotics
transaction, you also die as McCloud did. They make an
example of you. They tie your hands behind your back
and shoot you. Your coffin is the trunk of an Oldsmobile
98," Binh said.

Please, Kiet thought, no reminiscences. "I would like you to examine the Caribou, McCloud's belongings, and his room at the Continental."

"Fingerprints too, of course."

"Of course." He pictured Binh's forensic team, as he termed them, coating the entire interior of the aircraft with white powder. Kiet stopped himself from reminding his adjutant that Luong had no fingerprint registry. "Check, too, employees of Associate Deputy Minister Min who are living beyond their salaries."

"They *all* do, Superintendent."

"Then narrow it to the most blatantly affluent, please. I would guess that a murder conspiracy pays better than temporary loss of vision when a suitcase is being searched."

"And order an autopsy?"

Binh had brought home some odd ideas about police work. The medical examiner system was one. But for the suspicion of poisoning, the condition of a corpse was ample indication of foul play, was it not? McCloud's cockpit had been redecorated with his blood. Suicide and heart seizure could be eliminated as causes of death. From that point you investigated and listened to rumors and gossip, of which Hickorn was rife. Then you apprehended the killer, gave him a trial, and blindfolded him in front of sandbags.

Kiet said nothing.

"When I was in Washington, we had one case that was an apparent suicide," Binh said. "A single gunshot wound to the victim's temple. The pistol was in his hand. An open-and-shut case, right?"

"Yes," Kiet said, certain that it was not.

"The autopsy disclosed that the victim, an elderly gentleman whose considerable estate was in dispute by greedy relatives, suffered so from arthritis and bursitis that it would have been impossible for him to hold the pistol at the required angle.''

''Interesting.''

''A stepson who was to be written out of the will was arrested the following day,'' Binh said happily.

Kiet nodded his head reluctantly. An autopsy, then, for Denny McCloud, making him the dubious procedure's first customer.

3

SUPERINTENDENT KIET WAS uncomfortable in foreign embassies, particularly those of the superpowers. Discomfort in the United States Embassy was magnified by its climate. At least the Soviets' air conditioning malfunctioned regularly, sputtering and crackling, and once during a visit failing altogether in an unseen clap of manmade thunder and a subsequent stench of ozone and leaking freon gas.

Here, though, in Ambassador Smithson's inner reception area, it was like being in a refrigerator. Kiet's perspiration had formed a patina of frost, adhering clothing to skin. He wondered if they recruited foreign service personnel solely from their arctic provinces of Alaska and Minnesota.

Kiet had hoped to do his business with a clerk charged with passports and the comings and goings of American citizens. But the day had begun badly and again good fortune eluded him. Somebody had informed Ambassador Smithson of his presence and Smithson insisted on seeing him.

Smithson came out of his office and said, smiling, "Superintendent, how nice. Come in, come in."

Kiet was wary of such enthusiasm and good cheer in this serious and reserved man. The ambassador was lean and gray-maned. He had the posture of a monument. His membership in an American power clique known as Ivy League Eastern Establishment had somehow conferred

11

him with the ability to wear three-piece pinstripes in Hickorn's ninety-degree temperatures and ninety-percent humidity without sweating a droplet. Further, it allowed him to dress casually in shirtsleeves as he was now, oblivious to an environment best suited for polar bears.

Kiet missed Ritchie, the former ambassador. Ritchie's concerns were human rights and political prisoners, of which Kiet had none. After Kiet convinced him that his jail contained only generic criminals, they got along grandly. Smithson was much more difficult to comprehend. His avowed goal in Luong was to thwart a communist menace that did not exist. Luong Rouge insurgents were sporadically active in the highlands, as they had been for years, setting the occasional ambush, essentially making nuisances of themselves. Smithson insisted that guerrilla activity was "escalating," soon to sweep into the cities and destroy democracy.

"Look at this, Kiet," Smithson said, gesturing at his desktop computer. "We just installed it. I had to show you. State of the art. This integrated system will process and store various embassy functions, keep track of our citizens in the country, and interface with intelligence operations. Data from satellites can be pulled up with a few keystrokes."

"Spy satellites, Mr. Ambassador? Electronic voyeurs?"

"Yes, indeed. Henceforth, we will be able to detect large-scale Rouge troop movements."

Splendid, Kiet thought. A magical gadget whizzing around in outer space, snooping for guerrillas who did their mischief in bands of twenty or less. "I am impressed, sir. May I have a demonstration, please?"

"Of course, but first I would like to convey to you how delighted I am about the military action last week in the highlands and how it impacted the Rouge's latest offensive."

Kiet, who had nothing whatsoever to do with it, thanked him. He had heard of the clash secondhand and the results puzzled him. Encounters between the military and the Rouge on the remote trails northwest of Obon were infrequent, and seldom produced casualties, but nine Rouge guerrillas had been killed by Royal Luongan Army soldiers. Even stranger was the location of the battle—ten kilometers from the nearest government installation.

Ambassador Smithson cocked a thumb at a framed photograph on the wall behind his desk, a likeness of Brigadier General Chi Vo, commander of the Second Military District in Obon. "A damned fine trooper," he said, winking. "That victory should silence his critics once and for all. Ril Thoi and his Rouge will rue the day they locked horns with Vo. Unfortunately, I rarely have the opportunity to see him, since his efforts against the communists and the drug traffickers keep his nose to the old grindstone. This is a general whose priorities are straight."

Kiet smiled politely and closed his eyes, thinking: Naturally Vo remains in Obon. How else can he protect his opium profits from greedy subordinates, who would rob and connive against him the instant he left?

"As far as I'm concerned, Vo interdicted the beginning of a major build-up."

"Yes, sir."

Smithson winked again. "I was posted in Saigon in the 1960s. I know how these situations develop. I can easily conceptualize a Tet Offensive in the making."

"Yes, sir."

The ambassadorial cocked thumb moved to a picture on Vo's immediate right, a photo of Lieutenant Colonel Marsad Ref, Vo's chief of staff. It was smaller and mounted a bit lower. There was a chain-of-command symmetry to Luongans impaled in this office, highlighted by a huge color print of His Royal Highness on the opposite wall. Prince Novisad Pakse smiled serenely above crossed flags of the host and guest nations.

"That little fellow is a tiger," Smithson said admiringly. "He personally led the firefight, you know."

Kiet knew. And he knew Marsad Ref as well as he cared to. Vo's pet colonel glowered at the camera, sporting the mirrored aviator sunglasses he wore indoors and out. Ref was cruel and ambitious. He stood with a polished boot on the corpse of a Luong Rouge, like a sportsman who had bagged a record kill.

"Other news, Superintendent, more up your alley. It appears that we might secure permission to resume defoliation. Prince Pakse and Minister of Defense Van seem enthusiastic. I don't have to jog your memory on how successful a similar operation was two years ago, do I?"

Indeed not. Kiet wondered who was up for reelection back home. In the previous foray, Luongan troops and American DEA agents were helicoptered to the highlands, where they hacked down and burned fifty acres of poppy plants. A week later, eighty-seven pounds of opium gum was conveniently seized at Hickorn International by Lon Min and his customs inspectors. If the war against Luongan heroin wasn't yet over, a decisive battle had been won. Smithson confirmed this personally to Kiet by showing him videotapes of television newscasts of the story narrated by celebrity journalists named Tom Rather and Dan Brokaw. Shortly thereafter, a supplemental American foreign-aid grant provided for the refurbishment of National Stadium. And that was that.

"We're entering a glorious period," Smithson went on. "Keep this under your hat, but Prince Pakse is presiding over an upcoming ceremony where Avenue Mao Tse-tung is being renamed Avenue Ronald Reagan.

Kiet feigned surprise. He had already been asked to plan security for the event. His Royal Highness's neutralist policy was centered on the naming and renaming of Hickorn streets in honor of prominent foreigners, dead and alive. If some ridiculed it as buffoonery, so be it. If the ridicule extended to his gradual withdrawal from public life in favor of his true passion—pocket billiards—let them whisper and snicker of senility.

But don't do it to Bamsan Kiet's face. You would be reminded in harsh terms that the last foreign flag to fly in Hickorn, aside from those over embassies and consulates, was the French tricolor three decades past.

"Mr. Ambassador, the computer demonstration, please."

"I'm sorry, Kiet, I do depart on tangents, don't I? How about an example of our data base capabilities? There are roughly three hundred Americans now in Hickorn. Let me give you an exact fig—"

"Pardon me, Mr. Ambassador. Information on one American in particular, if you will. A Denny or Dennis McCloud."

Smithson looked at him. "The name doesn't ring a bell, but let's see what we can do."

The ambassador seemed to Kiet childlike as he typed. "Here we are! McCloud, Dennis Duane. Age 43. 6'1", 220 pounds. Unmarried. Born in Seattle. Graduated from high school, attended junior college for two years. Enlisted in the army, obtained a commission through Officer Candidate School, attended flight school and qualified in fixed-wing aircraft. Assigned to Vietnam. Hmm, volunteered for extension of duty at USMACV. Received honorable discharge in Saigon at rank of captain. Flew for hire in different parts of the world. Uganda, Angola, Indonesia, Venezuela. Moved to Australia in the late 1970s. Still maintains a residence there. Worked in Thailand off and on in the early 80s. Bought a surplus twin-engine de Havilland Caribou, came to Luong with it, and opened a freight and charter business, Luong Express. Resides at the Hickorn Continental Hotel. Oh—"

"Sir?"

"The remaining information is in the nature of confidential inquiries, Superintendent."

"I am the police, sir. While the people of Hickorn have a much-deserved reputation for gossip, I am capable of keeping a secret."

"Nobody implied that you are not, but this is a civil matter, not a criminal one. I doubt if you would be interested."

"I would be appreciative, Mr. Ambassador."

"Very well. I see no harm. We have received complaints of overdue bills from McCloud's Hickorn creditors, and the firm that finances his airplane wishes us to persuade him to get up-to-date on his payments. The financial institution is in Australia, so repossession would be a cumbersome proposition, to say the least."

"Did you intercede in behalf of McCloud's creditors, sir?"

"No. Per Luongan law, we have no actual authority over our citizens in civil disputes. This is an embarrassing situation, though. If the complaints continue, we'll counsel McCloud and convey the message that while he is not an employee of the United States of America, he is in effect a representative and should conduct himself with integrity and honor."

From what Kiet knew of McCloud, he doubted if such a flatulent approach would have persuaded him to behave responsibly. McCloud's indebtedness surprised him. Lon Min said he spent money freely, but surely he had an opium connection and his army charter contract could not have been anything but bloated. "Mr. Ambassador, does your computer mention a flying contract with the Royal Luongan Army?"

Smithson squinted at the green screen. "There is no indication."

"Apparently McCloud was a mercenary in every sense of the word."

"Was? Past tense? Incidentally, why are you asking me about Mr. Mc—"

The screen flickered and went blank. Smithson punched keyboard buttons, punched them hard. "I don't understand this, Superintendent."

Kiet did understand. All he knew of computers was that Hickorn's erratic electrical output disabled them fast. Gifts of the devices to his department from the French and Soviets moldered in storage, dead as Kiet's ancestors. Western technological fallibility delighted him. "A temporary problem, I'm sure," he said.

Smithson punched more buttons, cuffed the side of the monitor, then gave up with a sigh. "Yes, temporary. Now why, Kiet, the questions regarding Dennis McCloud?"

"He was murdered last night. We have few details and the killer has not been apprehended. Naturally, I will notify you of developments on the case."

Smithson blanched. Kiet rose before he could reply. He ended the visit with a farewell that was as popular to Americans as tomato catsup on their food: "Have a nice day, Mr. Ambassador."

4

THE HICKORN CONTINENTAL Hotel was south and west
of the United States Embassy, whose south cross street
was Avenue Irving Crane, named in homage to His Royal
Highness's favorite billiards shooter. In the intersection
circle stood a bronze statue of Prince Savhana, romanti-
cally savage atop a rearing horse, sword in hand. Prince
Savhana and his soldiers had repelled a Chinese invasion
one and a half centuries before the birth of Jesus of
Nazareth. The battle was the Kingdom of Luong's last
military triumph.

Then came Avenue Mao Tse-tung, soon to be Avenue
Ronald Reagan. Kiet knew that the redesignation would
be popular in Hickorn; the Chinese had occupied Luong
in the fifteenth through the eighteenth centuries and
hostility toward them had barely diminished. Next was
Avenue John F. Kennedy, and one block to the west, at
the intersection of Rue Ho Chi Minh, the Continental.

Kiet walked the four blocks. Midday was nearing and
downtown Hickorn was alive with commerce. Sidewalks
were clogged with shoppers and vendors, who haggled
noisily over the price of produce, meats, and clothing.
Bicycles, pedicabs, and a smattering of automobiles
challenged one another and pedestrians on the streets.
Since the days of carriages and ox carts, Luongans in
vehicles believed their right to reach a destination by the
most direct route was preeminent. He smiled, remembering Binh's astonishment at the rigid structure of Washing-

18

ton, D.C.'s traffic, the signal lights and the stop signs
and the policemen diverted from crimebusting to enforce
driving regulations.

Kiet's stomach informed him that he had missed
breakfast. The stroll had spiked his appetite. What it
hadn't done was clear the contradictions of this case
from his head. McCloud perhaps dying slowly, his tortur-
ers rummaging the airplane for contraband they possibly
didn't find. McCloud presumably awash in money, yet
pursued by creditors. Airport workers blinded and de-
prived of hearing as if by biblical vengeance. Never
before had an investigation become so convoluted so
soon.

The Hickorn Continental was Luong's finest hotel. It
was four stories of stucco and tile roof, constructed in
the 1920s, and owned to this day by absentee French-
men. Western travel brochures boasted of its "sleepy
colonial ambience." Denny McCloud had not lived there
cheaply. The ground-level *terrasse* was an open-air res-
taurant. Its speciality was shrimp scraped from the floor
of the Ma San River, rushed to the Continental's kitchen,
and fried in peanut oil and sesame seeds.

On his third plate of the exquisite freshwater shellfish,
Kiet began to relax. Contributing to his mood was a
second bottle of Golden Tiger beer, a smooth local brew
curiously nicknamed "Amber Death" by visitors. He
saw Gaston LaCroix, the hotel manager, and waved him
over.

LaCroix had been a clerk for the last French governor
general, had married a Luongan woman, and had stayed
on after Independence. This antique expatriate had never
been caught breaking a law, but Kiet distrusted him
nonetheless. He distrusted any American or European
who went *engagé*. Why did they not yearn for their
homelands? What, after all, was so awful about the
country of one's birth? If Kiet were forced to leave

Luong for more than a month, he knew he would be a melancholy wreck.

LaCroix sat at Kiet's table and said, nervously, "This is a terrible tragedy, Superintendent, the murder of Mr. McCloud."

Kiet agreed that is was. "Have my men searched McCloud's room yet?"

'They have, Superintendent. They informed me of the killing and I accompanied them on their search. It shocked me to see that the room was completely empty."

LaCroix was thin and white-haired, dressed as always in a white suit. He struck Kiet as an emaciated version of his favorite Western actor, Sydney Greenstreet. "McCloud was embarking on a trip. His luggage was on the Caribou."

"Superintendent, not a single personal belonging remained in the room and his rent is current for another month. He paid me in advance two days ago. In cash."

Kiet hesitated. If McCloud's money problems were as serious as Ambassador Smithson's computer had stated, why was he so solid with LaCroix and Lon Min? "How much was his rent?"

"Since he was a permanent resident, I gave him a monthly rate at a substantial discount."

"The amount, please."

Gaston LaCroix cleared his throat. "Two thousand American dollars."

"All of which is reported by bookkeeping to your corporate masters in Paris, I presume."

LaCroix threw up bony hands. "Superintendent, these Americans, they demand so much! Hot water any time of the day and night. Daily maid service. Ceiling fans that are operational. My overhead is staggering."

Kiet smiled. This was a game he and LaCroix had played for years. Kiet did not care that LaCroix stole from his owners. He *did* care that LaCroix was once more on the verge of playing coy. Affluent travelers lodged at the Continental. Affluent residents, Luongans and foreigners alike, ate and drank there. LaCroix's ear was sensitive, his capacity for gossip encyclopedic. "Please reminisce with me about Denny McCloud. Tell me everything you know. Bore me with each trivial detail. I have the time."

"Superintendent, the privacy of my guests is sacrosanct. I do not pry."

Kiet finished his meal, patted his lips with his napkin, and stretched, his eyes locked throughout on LaCroix, who refused to return his gaze.

"The shrimp were wonderful."

"Thank you, Superintendent."

"You know, my top assistant, Captain Binh, studied police science in America."

"Captain Binh is an extremely capable young man," LaCroix said. "He and you and your entire department are a credit to our city."

"Binh regales me with fantastic stories of his experiences in the District of Columbia. On one assignment he rode in a car with officers who were frustrated by a particular café. They were certain that the restaurateur was selling illegal drugs, but they could never catch him in the act.

"Do you know what they did? They arranged to have him ticketed by public health authorities for sanitation violations and padlocked his doors. He no longer had a convenient means of selling his drugs. Ingenious, don't you agree, LaCroix?"

LaCroix replied by fidgeting in his chair.

"Coincidentally, as I arrived here today for your marvelous shrimp, I passed your kitchen and saw flies buzzing about. Dirty, filthy flies. I am confident that we have

21

sanitation laws that similarly apply. It is only a matter of digging deeply enough in the ordinance book.''

"Superintendent, this is Hickorn, not Paris! *All* kitchens have flies.''

Kiet made a swirling motion with a fingertip. ''Buzz, buzz. Dirty, filthy.''

LaCroix leaned forward and whispered, ''I cannot help but notice things, Superintendent. My duties require me to be at the Continental for long hours. In the evenings, McCloud was a frequent patron of the *terrasse*. He enjoyed good whiskey and the companionship of friends.''

"That is no secret, LaCroix. Why are we whispering?''

LaCroix's voice dropped to a hiss. ''He entertained important people. Names that I would really not care to mention. They would not appreciate my—''

"May I guess, please? Army officers?''

"Yes, usually. And when drinks were served, McCloud paid for them.''

"Were your hostesses invited to linger at McCloud's parties?''

LaCroix smirked. ''Superintendent, these are normal, virile men. They enjoy the company of lovely ladies.''

LaCroix's hostesses were young Luongans who wore skin-tight dresses slit at the sides in a style referred to as Suzy Wong. They painted their faces with mascara and lipstick and rouge. Some had had eyelid surgery, giving them the ''round eye'' look prized by their clients. Kiet wondered what agony their mothers and fathers endured, how many nights the clown faces of their daughters appeared in dreams.

"If a hostess and an officer developed a friendship, would McCloud then make it possible for them to go upstairs?''

"My hostesses are under no such obligation. I employ

22

them to refill drinks and encourage a congenial atmosphere. If an attraction occurs . . . I cannot supervise each of my people every minute of every day.''

Kiet groaned and closed his eyes. LaCroix and his girls split fifty-fifty. Rooms taken during a hostess's shift were surcharged, the additional rent going into LaCroix's pocket. "The ordinance book,'' Kiet reminded him. "Your whores are Luong's most beauteous. They are not street tramps. I have no desire to enforce obscure prostitution laws.''

"Superintendent, I am cooperating.''

"And I am investigating a murder, LaCroix. You are forcing me to draw words from your mouth one by one. Names, please.''

"I don't know them well. They're from Obon, Second Military District officers, captains and majors and colonels. I can tell an Obon soldier from a Hickorn soldier by my ears. At a distance of fifty meters. They're so isolated up there, they explode with joy when they come to town. Not that they're any trouble. Broken glasses are inexpensive to replace. They're quite generous and gracious when they return the following day to pay for damage. McCloud would fly them down and take them out for a night of fun.''

"What sort of person was Denny McCloud? Did you like him?''

"I'm not one to speak ill of the departed, but I wouldn't invite him to my home, no. He slapped everyone on the back and had a—how do we say it?—horselaugh. He was the loudest of the loud. If it were possible to awaken someone from the dead, McCloud could resurrect himself with his normal tone of voice.''

"You tolerated him for his money, though.''

"I am a businessman,'' LaCroix said firmly. "He paid me what he owed and did not quibble.''

"An admirable recommendation," Kiet said. "Did he have guests other than the army hangers-on?"

"For the last three or four weeks, an American woman. With her he was subdued. Smitten, if you will. They met here once or twice a week for dinner and cocktails. Sometimes they went to his room afterwards, sometimes elsewhere. He wasn't the same person with her, Superintendent. He held her hand and spoke too softly to be overheard."

Kiet withdrew a notebook from his shirt pocket. "Her name?"

"Susan. I honestly cannot supply you a last name. McCloud did not introduce us formally. He obviously preferred to separate her from his other life. She is a student visiting Luong for research. I know that much. She has big Caucasian breasts. This late in life, Superintendent, I still miss my France for its women and those soft globes."

"All right," Kiet said. "Before I set my vice squad after your prostitutes, I will give you another chance to identify the Obon soldiers."

"You have a vice squad, Superintendent?"

"My Captain Binh would love to initiate the unit. As part of his training, he served for six weeks with a vice squad in the United States capital. He loved the continuous activity."

"Colonel Ref."

"Lieutenant Colonel Marsad Ref, General Vo's chief of staff?"

"Superintendent, you criticize me for whispering and not speaking directly. Ref is terrifying. If he knew that—"

"He won't."

"He has ways."

"LaCroix, I've solved every murder in Hickorn since my appointment as superintendent."

"My ghost will thank you."

"He and McCloud were close?"

"Very. When they were together by themselves, their conversations were as intimate as McCloud's with the Susan woman."

"Why are you so afraid of him?"

"My hostesses tell me to be. He hurts them."

5

KIET RETURNED TO Police Headquarters—two stories of massive doors and blockish, unadorned stucco that had been barracks and a command center for Hickorn-based Legionnaires. The interior was spare and cold, little changed from the days of French hegemony. Boots on hallway tile produced echoes and the rooms smelled of musty permanence. Kiet liked the businesslike message the place gave to both his policemen and their reluctant guests.

The address of Headquarters was 900 Avenue Alexandre Loubet, a street named for a nineteenth-century priest who took time from saving pagan souls to romanize the Luongan language. Prince Pakse, a Catholic, had never tampered with its designation. IIis subjects were evenly divided between Buddhists and Christians, and the exchange of religious views had not always been peaceful. Thus an undercurrent existed that His Royal Highness was wise not to inflame. Early in adulthood, Kiet made a logical compromise and entered the undemanding faith of agnosticism. It spared him café debates on the merits of unseen deities, and more important, it spared him enemies.

On his desk was a message to either himself or Captain Binh from Dr. Pho, Binh's medical examiner. Kiet groaned. The autopsy on Denny McCloud was completed and Binh wasn't around. Kiet would be expected to call on the good doctor and be treated to a description of each and every wound that contributed to McCloud's death.

Dr. Pho was Hickorn's only pathologist. He was also an entrepreneur, owner of a mortuary situated on the corner of Avenue Ché Guevara and Richard Nixon Boulevard. This was the most ironic intersection in the city, the figurative collision of a communist martyr and a man who gained prominence with a bucket of red paint and a wide brush. But when Kiet entered Blessed Sleep Funeral Home, his mind was not on politics. Uppermost was the hope that Pho wasn't the kind of prideful craftsman who would insist on a demonstration of his skills. A verbal summary would suffice, thank you.

The anteroom of Blessed Sleep was appropriately somber: subdued lighting, dark woods, heavy furniture, and a brownish maroon carpet much too close to the hue of dried blood. Funeral music wafted at low volume from hidden speakers. It was an effective environment. Pho sold costly caskets and elaborate services whenever possible, Kiet knew. If he were a relative responsible for arrangements, he would sign any contract just to flee.

Dr. Pho greeted Kiet. He was an older gentleman, lean and gray, dressed in black slacks, white shirt, black tie, and a white smock speckled with unpleasant stains. He shook Kiet's hand. In his other he held a small envelope.

"Superintendent Kiet. You are prompt."

"This is a murder investigation, Doctor. What do you have for us, please?"

Dr. Pho frowned. "No living creature should pass on as Mr. McCloud did. He endured precisely thirty-seven stabbings, but only the thrust that drove through the rib cage into the heart was immediately fatal. The others were relatively superficial. Eventually he may have bled to death from them, but it is my opinion that the attack was not initially designed to kill. Dennis McCloud was tortured."

"Tortured to obtain information?" Kiet asked politely, wondering why he was abusing himself by remaining in a living mausoleum, listening to the obvious.

"I cannot tell you *why* he was tortured, Superintendent. Contusions on the torso and face lead me to speculate that a fistfight or blows from a blunt object partially disabled Mr. McCloud prior to the lacerations. If you would care to view the deceased—"

Dr. Pho was moving toward an inner door. Kiet stood fast. "No, no. After an autopsy has been accomplished by a pathologist with your credentials? No, that isn't necessary. Not at all. If you say torture, I accept torture."

"My conclusions aren't entirely based on tissue evidence, Superintendent. Excuse me for encroaching into your profession, but these influenced what I am telling you."

Dr. Pho tore the flap on the envelope and poured into Kiet's hand four red stones. They were transparent and faceted, each the size of a toenail.

Kiet went to the front windows. "My apologies to any vampires on the premises, Doctor," he said, pulling open the thick draperies and flooding the dim room with daylight.

Pho did not respond to the humor.

Kiet put on his reading glasses and held up one of the jewels. "Magnificient color and brilliance. Such a deep red. Are they rubies?"

"I don't know. I am a physician. I can identify kidney stones, but I am ignorant of gemstones."

"Where did you mine these?"

"I nearly didn't. I saw no good reason for a complete work-up. The man had been butchered. What else was there to know? Captain Binh insisted. He ordered me to be thorough. He lectured me on the procedures of American pathologists and how they uncovered subtle clues by paying meticulous attention to detail. Frankly, Superintendent, I was insulted. Binh is a layman and he was instructing me—"

"Yes, yes. Where, please?"

"In the lower intestines."

An image of Denny McCloud, cold and stiff and disemboweled on Pho's slab, flashed out of nowhere. Kiet took a deep breath and managed to erase it. "Could you estimate when McCloud swallowed the—whatever they are?"

"Ten to twelve hours before his death," Dr. Pho said. "I am certain of the time range because of the progress of the jewels in the victim's alimentary canal."

So McCloud had taken this bad meal before he departed Obon, Kiet thought. A treacherous and fatal snack. Kiet's opium theory was repudiated, his resistance to forensic medicine shown to be old-fashioned and stubborn and silly.

Kiet would congratulate Binh on his perceptiveness. Binh would refuse the praise, giving full credit to Kiet for permitting that this enhancement of police science be made available to the Hickorn Police Department. There would be no loss of face. The investigation could then progress.

Not that it would be smooth and easy. Conventional thinking and history dictated opium as a more evident motive for McCloud's murder. The geology of Luong was poor. No precious minerals had ever been taken from its crust and gem smuggling was unknown in Hickorn. Unfortunately, therefore, the store of information on opium trafficking and its principals was, irrelevant. The four red beauties might as well have arrived in McCloud's guts via flying saucer.

Circumstances *had* given Kiet an advantage and he recognized it: right now just two people on earth knew of the stones' whereabouts. He sifted them from palm to palm, saying, "One, two, three, four. This could be a fortune. Look at the size of them, Doctor."

Dr. Pho smiled. "I know what you are implying. There are no other stones. I am reasonably honest and I am most decidedly a coward. I am retiring within the year and I intend to live to enjoy it. I'm not naïve, Superintendent Kiet. The people seeking these won't give up until they die and everybody in their path dies."

"I'm not questioning your honor, Doctor," Kiet lied, fairly certain that Pho was telling the truth. "I am pleased that you realize the perils of the case."

"When we're finished with this interview, I'm going to reassemble Mr. McCloud, embalm him, and provide a suit of clothing at my own expense. If you will release the body, I'll immediately schedule the cremation service. The fee I can charge for cremation is low and there is hardly any profit. I discourage it usually, but the sooner McCloud is gone from Blessed Sleep, the safer I'll feel."

"Cremation?"

"That is what she requested. She said McCloud's preference was cremation."

"Who requested?"

"The woman who came to see me less than an hour ago. A distraught Occidental lady. She said that McCloud had no kin and that she was his dearest friend. She said that she had an appointment with the deceased at his hotel yesterday evening. When he wasn't there she became concerned. She returned to the Continental this morning and learned of his death. She asked to view the remains. In his present condition I of course refused. Not to mention that I was aware of it being a police matter."

"Her name?"

Dr. Pho went to his office and came back with a small

card. "It's an unusual name and I want to be sure I have it right. Susan Dempsey-Mohn."

"Where can I find her?"

"She did not offer an address. She paid cash. American dollars. I had no need to inquire. I don't keep records unless the bereaved applies for credit."

Kiet thought of LaCroix's soft globes. He pocketed the stones, anxious to depart and locate the Susan woman. "Confidentiality, Doctor?"

"You don't have to swear me to secrecy," Dr. Pho said in a soft voice and with eyes that did not leave Kiet's. "This conversation never happened and those evil rocks don't exist."

6

KIET'S IMPULSE WAS to stop at the American Embassy again. By now, a miracle might have raised Ambassador Smithson's computer from the dead. If not, perhaps a clerk could provide a manila folder and paper on the subject of Susan Dempsey-Mohn. Perhaps not. The anguish on Smithson's face when his green screen went stupid led Kiet to believe that considerable data had been transferred to and lost forever on magnetic plastic known as software. Even if the lobotomy rendered to the magical machinery by Hickorn Metropolitan Power and Light was not permanent, Kiet wasn't up to the ordeal. His nose was stuffy, a cold coming on. The climate of that icebox may prevent spoilage of dressed livestock, but a second visit so soon would land him in the hospital with pneumonia. There were investigative techniques less detrimental to one's health. If he didn't freeze to death, Smithson would finish him off with boredom.

Kiet guessed from his clerk's leer that the hunt had ended before it really began. The young uniformed patrolman made a sweeping hourglass motion and told him that a lady was waiting in his office, a lady who refused to identify herself and would speak only to the boss.

Kiet went in and shut the door behind him. The woman rose from a chair and extended her arm. "Superintendent, I'm Susan Dempsey-Mohn."

Luongan women did not exchange handshakes with men. Custom decreed it aggressive and offensive. Kiet accepted her hand tentatively. She was beautiful, for a Caucasian, he decided after a moment's study. In the days when attractive, sensual women were a larger part of his life, he had preferred them dusky and petite, in traditional silk dresses, their hair wrapped tightly in buns, cinched with gold barrettes.

Susan Dempsey-Mohn was the antithesis. She was nearly as tall as he, and her blond hair fell below her shoulders. She had blue eyes and rimless glasses. Her skin was as dark as a Luongan's, though its tone was strange, a result, it appeared, of prolonged exposure to the sun. She wore shorts, which abbreviated the longest legs Kiet had ever seen. Underneath her sleeveless top was nothing but Susan Dempsey-Mohn. Both articles of clothing and her gymnasium shoes too were printed with the names of their manufacturers.

A lusty and well-nourished female statue, yes, but her eyes were red from tears and she trembled. Kiet gave her tissues from a box on his desk and helped her resume her seat.

"Thank you," she said, balling the tissue in a fist. "I'm fresh out of tears, but just give me an hour."

"I'm sorry about Mr. McCloud. You and he were friends, I'm told."

"More than friends."

"That too, I've gathered."

"Who could have killed him, Superintendent? Dennis got along with everybody. He was a warm and outgoing person. Everyone liked him."

McCloud the jolly backslapper. Life of the party, generous with liquor and LaCroix's roundheeled hostesses. McCloud the shadowy hustler who reached too deeply into the pie and couldn't retrieve his paw in time. Kiet stepped around her affirmation and asked, "What is your business in Luong, please?"

"I'm a student. I have a six-month visa. Oh, I can't

prove it. It's in my apartment. I'm doing field research for my doctoral dissertation. It's entitled: The Kingdom of Luong, A Monarchical Third-World Anachronism. My advisor thinks it has a chance of being published. Not very many scholarly papers have been written on Luong.''

Kiet despised the term Third World. It was to him a child branded as a waif. "A college student? You've traveled far for your research project. Clarify your surname, if you will. You are American, yet it's hyphenated like a Britisher's.''

"Dempsey is my maiden name," she said. "My husband's was Mohn. It's not common, but it's done. It seemed criminal to me to have a name I'd carried with me for twenty-five years obliterated by a wedding ceremony.''

Kiet stared at her. "You have a husband? He's in Hickorn with you?''

"I'm sorry, no. We're divorced. He was an attorney and I worked as director of human resources for a commercial construction company. When our marriage dissolved, we sold the condo. I got half of that and the joint savings account. I sat down one evening and counted my assets and job satisfaction and satisfaction with life in general. Job satisfaction was zero, life in general not much higher. I've been fascinated with the Far East since I was a child and there are worse jobs than teaching at the Far Eastern department of a university. I gave my notice the next morning and cashed in my IRA and 401k. I was set for five years if I didn't squander my nest egg. I enrolled in grad school, got my master's, was approved for the doctoral program, and here I am.''

Her soliloquy caused Kiet to question his fluency in English. "A director of human resources does what?''

"It's an overblown title for personnel manager. I interviewed job applicants. I had input in dismissals that went to committee and I coordinated company benefit packages. It was a stress factory.''

Kiet nodded. ''That is part of what I do. I hire and fire and I am the committee. How, please, did you meet Mr. McCloud?''

It was one month ago last Wednesday. I was running.''

''You were running from somebody?''

''No.''

''You were late?''

''No, I was just running.''

Kiet looked at her.

''I run five miles every other morning.''

Then it struck him. He regularly read the overseas edition of *Time* magazine. He should have made the connection earlier. Susan Dempsey-Mohn was a member of that peculiar American subspecies known as Yuppie. ''I think I understand. Please continue.''

''My route takes me by the Continental. On mornings when Dennis ate breakfast there, we said hello as I passed. The American community in Hickorn is small. You greet one another whether you're acquainted or not. One day he held up a stop sign he'd hand-drawn on a napkin. It was colored red and was hex-shaped, just like the real ones. He'd put some effort into it. I thought it was cute. I stopped. He invited me to have breakfast with him.''

''You saw him frequently thereafter?''

A single tear formed in one eye. She dabbed it with a tissue. ''Yes.''

''My apologies if I'm being too personal, but your background is rather different from Mr. McCloud's.''

''It happened so fast that I still haven't been able to analyze my feelings. Opposites attract, et cetera, maybe. Dennis wasn't like any man I'd ever known. I come from a world where the height of excitement to a man is making the quarterfinals of his club's squash tournament or selling at thirty a stock he bought last year at twenty. Dennis has had airplanes shot out from under him. He drank cocktails with an African dictator thirty minutes before a rival faction stormed the palace. Dennis escaped down a balcony. He speaks seven languages and has lived on every continent except Antarctica. I could write theses in exotic places for the rest of my life and never experience a fraction of what he had. And, well, he was a hunk.''

Kiet conceded that McCloud had lived a zesty life, but he wondered how much was embellishment. Soldier-of-fortune types he had known shared a liking for liquor and wild stories. By the time they reached McCloud's age their brains were too mushy to distinguish truth from a lurid adventure novel. McCloud may have recited chapters to this ripe beauty and convinced himself that they were fact. Kiet made a mental note to look up the word ''hunk.''

"Did he discuss his flying business with you?''

Susan said, ''Broadly. He couldn't talk specifically about his government contract, which was the bulk of his work. He did say that he was vitally involved in a stepped-up effort against the Luong Rouge and the drug trade. He was so thrilled to be able to contribute, he didn't care that much about the money.''

She loved her Dennis McCloud, Kiet thought. She loved the image he projected, an image as thin as his napkin sketch. She had no inkling if either were real. Kiet's McCloud *was* real, eviscerated in Dr. Pho's morgue, the essence of his moral values sifted from his bowels. Kiet felt bad for her. ''Did he ever introduce you to his army colleagues?''

"No. He said it was too dangerous. The Rouge and the opium gangs weren't pleased about the added pressure against them.''

One mark on the positive side of McCloud's ledger, Kiet thought. "Had you and he made permanent plans?"

She sighed. "I asked him to move in with me. He made excuses. A night or two a week we'd stay at the Continental, a night or two we'd go to my apartment. He loved me too, but it wasn't in his makeup to be pinned down and, as he put it, fitted with a ball and chain. I know what's going through your head. He was an elusive fish who kept slipping the hook. That was part of his charm. Could be, but me and my subconscious haven't been speaking."

It wasn't going through Kiet's head, but it nevertheless made sense. "Susan, we have no clues from his airplane or his hotel room. I need to search your apartment."

"Why? Am I a suspect?"

"Absolutely not. But Dennis McCloud was there. I have no chance of solving his murder unless I go where he has recently been."

"I have a razor of his and a toothbrush and some underwear. If those are clues—"

"I would be grateful."

"You could obtain a search warrant from a judge, I suppose."

"I have search warrant forms in my desk."

"The police can authorize a search?"

"Luongan law. Judges are too busy dispensing justice to be troubled."

"Wow," Susan said. "I've been concentrating on history and geography. I haven't gotten to your criminal justice system."

"It is straightforward," Kiet said.

"I don't live far. We could walk."

"How far, please?"

"On Avenue Charles de Gaulle, two streets from the river."

Eight blocks from 900 Avenue Alexandre Loubet, Kiet estimated.

"We'll take the Citroën," he said.

Susan Dempsey-Mohn lived in a clean neighborhood of Luongan merchants, bureaucrats, and middle-class Westerners who could not afford opulent villas in the International District. Her apartment was on the second floor of three. It had a balcony, an all-purpose room, and a private toilet. The flat was sparsely furnished and tidy.

"The hardest thing to get used to was the hot water", she said as she ushered Kiet in. "There's no heater. Water's hot only until it's gone through the pipes on the roof. I've taught myself to take a shower in ninety seconds. That and the geckos crawling around on the ceiling."

"You don't kill them, do you? They're harmless."

"I was tempted until Dennis told me about their appetite for insects."

"May I?"

"Feel free, but there isn't much to prowl through."

An hour later, Kiet believed her. Susan's apartment contained only clothing, kitchenware, books and writing material, and innocuous personal articles. When he was done and ready to leave, he noticed a blank look on her face. He read it as the forerunner of a breakdown and said, "Please lie down and try to sleep. You'll feel better."

"No, I'm fine. It's just a creepy feeling I have that someone else has been here. I'm a neat, organized person—I border on fussy. I'd swear my clothing is stacked out of order. Same with the notepads and reference books on my desk. It could be my imagination, but I don't think so."

"Does anyone besides you have a key?"

"With the exception of the manager, no. Not even Dennis did."

Kiet thanked her for her indulgence and promised to be in touch when there were developments in the case. He went downstairs to the building manager's unit. An elderly wrinkled woman who came up to his chest answered. She had on the traditional silk pajamas that Luongan women wore for everyday activities. Her teeth were blackened from decades of chewing betel nut.

Kiet presented identification. The woman said her name was Lei. She aimed a gnarled finger upward and said, "You're here because of the American, aren't you?"

"I do need some information."

"Her man was stabbed to death. He was the one, wasn't he? She entertained him in her room all night, you know." Lei redirected the digit at Kiet. "If you lead a loose life it will have a bad ending."

Everyone knew, Kiet thought. Hickorn rumors exceeded the speed of light. "Did she have other male visitors?"

"None that I knew of. To be fair, she was pleasant and paid her rent on time."

"Then aren't you being overly harsh, Madame? In my opinion, faithfulness to one lover doesn't make a woman loose."

"There's more. Have you a piece of paper?"

Kiet gave her his notebook. Slowly, she wrote scrawled letters and handed it back. "I find empty containers of this lotion in her trash."

Kiet read: sunscreen. "Your point, please."

"I never saw such lotion until Mrs. Dempsey-Mohn moved in. I asked her once what it was. She said it blocked out the sun's ultraviolet rays."

"The solution to your puzzle?"

"To avoid the sun's rays, you stay indoors at midday

when it is the hottest, don't you? Every sane Luongan rests."

Kiet nodded in agreement. "Westerners call it siesta."

"Mrs. Dempsey-Mohn didn't. She applied the cream and took a blanket to the roof, removed her robe, and lay there and roasted."

The *Time* article. Tanning. A Yuppie compulsion. Kiet recalled that during their icy winters they browned inside of machines in parlors dedicated to that sole purpose. "Eccentric, yes, but you haven't yet justified your hostility."

"She was naked," Lei said. 'Being alone and locking the door behind her doesn't make her a modest person. It doesn't make it right."

"Madame, I am more and more confused at what is right and what isn't. A final question. Did anybody visit Susan Dempsey-Mohn's apartment in the past twenty-four hours?"

"I saw no one. I am not a snooper."

Of course not, Kiet thought. Nobody in Hickorn snoops. He resisted asking how she knew that Susan sunbathed in the nude. He thanked her for her help and walked the stairs to the roof.

With an exception, the immediate neighborhood squatted below—apartments and markets and theaters no higher than two stories. Hickorn was flatter than Kiet's insteps. Its panorama spread before him.

The Ma San River was due north. Kiet saw Savhana Island and National Stadium thereon. The Americans had done a remarkable job renewing it. Bleacher sections were segmented in a rainbow of colors. The plastic grass they had insisted on laying mildewed instantly and was replaced by native turf that thrived. West of the Ma San, connected to the island and the mainland by iron bridges, was Foh Ten, a desperate slum otherwise known as

40

Dragon's Bile. From this vantage point, its tin and scrap-wood shacks had a nestled symmetry.

To the northeast, the Hickorn Continental dominated. East by northeast was the Royal Palace—pillared marble surrounded by emerald landscaping. Kiet turned around. Luong University was a kilometer south, its dormitories and lecture halls hidden by trees older than the French missionaries who founded it.

Bamsan Kiet loved his city. He treasured it in this moment of abstraction, standing too high and too distant to see its festering pockets.

He swiveled again and focused on the exception, the Soviet Embassy. The structure was gray, four stolid tiers of tiny, smoked windows capped by a thicket of antennas and a satellite dish. Ambassador Smithson had protested it as an espionage device. Kiet smiled, imagining the antennas making obscene gestures to the American space vehicles whenever they orbited overhead.

He savored the view for a short minute longer and started downstairs, bound for a festering pocket.

7

AVENUE DWIGHT EISENHOWER was a gaudy necklace of
shops that catered to those who could afford the best
and the latest. It originated at the waterfront and the chic
sidewalk cafés on Ma San Boulevard and leisured east to
the International District, the lode of its most loyal
customers. Luong's average per-capita income was $507
US; exclusivity was assured.

Anything from musty brandies to Scottish woolens to
twenty-carat-gold chain sold by the meter was available.
European designer labels were as common as dust. And
if one paid a substantial deposit, one could order a
Mercedes-Benz or a Jaguar and greet it at homeland
docks, sans local taxes. Goods and services that dared
not glimmer in showrooms could be acquired through
trust and connection and price on *Lé Avenue,* as patrons
with bulging pocketbooks had christened it.

Lé Avenue merchants were predominantly Indian and
Chinese. Engines of our economy, Kiet thought wryly,
swerving his Citröen into the only parking space in sight.
*Our Asian brothers tutor us on the art of commerce and
are thoughtful enough to control it for us.*

The store he sought exhibited in its windows slacks
and jackets and neckties. The cloth was of the highest
quality, the patterns and tones conservative. Price tags
were marked with staggering numbers. The BOMBAY
TAILORS sign over the doorway was a painted board,
small and subtle, almost humble. Kiet knew better.

He entered to the jittery and blinding smile of Mr. A. Singh, the proprietor. "Superintendent, it has been too long! How may I be of service? You are a man made for a silk ascot."

Singh was in his thirties, a short and swarthy man with no hard edges. His hair glistened and his eyes were liquid. Kiet regarded him as an adder. "I cannot pay your prices."

"Ah, but a sizable discount to a gentleman who protects us from hooligans is a just reward for devotion to duty."

"Mr. Singh, please remember that I refused your previous bribe offers. May we speak in privacy?"

Singh moved a shoulder, the gesture of a man without a choice. He led Kiet behind a curtain to a cramped room. Papers and invoices were piled haphazardly on a rolltop desk. An antique foot-treadle sewing machine was being used as a tea table. Singh sat in a folding chair. Kiet took another. He placed the four red stones on the sewing machine and said, "Please tell me what they are."

Singh picked them up one by one and examined them with an eyepiece. Kiet watched him closely. By the fourth stone, the Indian's hands were trembling.

"Superintendent, I am a tailor, not a jeweler. I think they are genuine rubies, but they could be synthetic. Some imitations are quite clever. You are my fine friend, however. I would be willing to take the risk and offer—"

"Mr. Singh, they are not for sale. This is police evidence, not a dowry. Please offer your expertise on their origin and value."

"I am honored that you deem me an authority, but—"

"*But* you are a nominal tailor, Singh. Your suits are ready-made from Italy and Hong Kong."

"Sir, I am a craftsman," Singh said, too defensive by now for the intended show of outrage to have any effect.

"A craftsman, yes, but a businessman first," Kiet said. "A businessman must be creative to survive the competition, mustn't he? A customer pays you money for a garment. I think your business must be more flexible and varied than that."

Singh caught the meaning and hesitated before answering. "While I will occasionally take in trade in lieu of cash on merchandise a particularly attractive bauble as a gift for my beloved wife, I am not a qualified gemologist."

Kiet sighed and looked at the ceiling. "Your primary business is money changing. Four hundred of our impotent Luongan zin equal a single U.S. dollar. That is the official rate given at banks and embassies. You trade zin at—what today?—six hundred-to-one in order to buy things you could not possibly buy with zin. If you aren't already aware, black-market money changing is illegal."

"Superintendent, the practice is condoned! It brings hard currency into our impoverished economy. It is a patriotic service to my country. Have you never changed dollars on the street?"

"No, never." Kiet lied. "And it has gone far enough. I'm contemplating a crackdown, with you made an example. The law is the law. Speak to me of these stones and of trends. The traffic in your shop qualifies you as Hickorn's foremost economist."

Mr. Singh nodded in defeat. "Very well. I am certain they are pigeon blood rubies."

"Pigeon blood?"

"Yes. They are named for their glorious color and are extremely rare. They're found exclusively in the Mogok Valley of Upper Burma. They're the most valuable gems on earth, worth more than the purest diamonds. These stones weigh five to seven carats apiece. The total value of the four could exceed a million American dollars.

"Socialist generals have ruled Burma since the 1960s.

They nationalized everything, including the ruby industry. As a consequence, private initiative was destroyed. Pigeon bloods all but vanished from government-sponsored auctions. The majority of rubies on the outside market are provided by independent third parties."

"By third parties do you mean smugglers who desire more than salaries paid in a socialist paradise to mine, cut, and sell rubies?"

"Yes. These were cut and polished in workshops hidden in the jungle. Their marginally professional faceting matters little. Diamonds are treasured for their brilliance. Rubies, emeralds, and sapphires are valued for their color. May I ask how these came into your possession?"

"No," Kiet said. "What is their usual route from Burma to their eventual owners?"

"Through the jungles to Thailand. They are either sold in Bangkok or are flown out in secret compartments and body cavities."

Kiet's next question was silent. He drummed fingers on the makeshift tea table and stared at Singh.

The tailor replied, "Of any person in Hickorn to bring me the first pigeon blood I've seen, I wouldn't have thought him to be you, Superintendent."

"It is a surprise to me too, Mr. Singh."

"There have been whispers. Bandits and soldiers in Burma and Thailand who confront smugglers demand tariffs, and the tariffs have increased. Thailand is paid by Western nations to make war against opium farmers and communists, as Luong is. They are sending increasing numbers of troops on helicopters and depositing them in no-man's-land. It gets crowded. Opportunities outside the parameters of missions agreed to on treaties develop. Soldiers throughout the world are underpaid and mistreated, Superintendent. Soldiers will do what soldiers do."

"Luong's northern frontier joins Upper Burma," Kiet

said, a picture forming. "The highlands isn't crowded. If you have the legs and the lungs and the heart for steep hills and forests and snakes and tigers and rain torrents, you could reach the outskirts of Obon without passing a soul."

"You could," Singh agreed. "Yes, you could. What I've said, however, is a whistling in the air."

"I know. Mere rumors. On a different subject, do you have a client named Denny McCloud?"

"I knew him casually. I was saddened by the news of his death."

"Unless I get to the bottom of this quickly, his ailment may prove contagious."

Singh flinched as if Kiet's statement had arrived via a fist. "Tea, Superintendent?"

"No, thank you. My ordinance book is closed, Singh. Play with zin and dollars and yen and francs until you're up to your neck in currency. I don't care. I'm looking for a killer."

"The rubies and Denny McCloud, in regard to the case, they're linked, aren't they? I don't anticipate a reply. The day before yesterday, McCloud telephoned and requested that I meet him after shop hours. I complied. I waited interminably. He knocked on the alley door at ten o'clock. I'm a devout family man. I was irritated at being kept in the shop so late."

"Was the inconvenience worth it?"

"Indeed."

"How much money was changed?"

"Five thousand American dollars. As you know, I routinely deal in larger sums, but this was a reverse transaction. Zin for dollars. Five million zin. The bills were in mixed denominations, some of them wadded up and some rubber-banded. Clearly, the cash had been accumulated over a period of time and stashed. We weren't finished counting until midnight. The unfortunate Mr. McCloud had no respect for legal tender, Superintendent."

"You paid him a thousand to one," Kiet said. "If he'd gone to a bank, he could have gotten, uh, about twelve thousand dollars. He paid you a seven-thousand-dollar bonus?"

"McCloud did not quibble. The bonus bought discretion."

And traveling money until he could convert the gems, Kiet thought. "Did he confide in you?"

"Any fool could see that he was departing Luong in haste. Denny McCloud was agitated and anxious, and he had been drinking. He was a physically strong and volatile man. He volunteered no information and I sought none. I'm neither a roughneck nor an idiot."

"What is the price of discretion for our chat, Singh?"

Kiet held the rubies in an open palm. Mr. A. Singh touched each with a fingertip and said, "The price has been paid by the chain of events, Superintendent. My life is dearer to me than the whole Mogok Valley."

8

IT COULD HAVE been the Golden Tiger beer he'd drunk with lunch or it could have been guilt over his hectoring of LaCroix and Singh or it could have been everything in general, but for whatever reason, Kiet's mouth was dry and his head was splitting. He resolved to stop drinking during the day. He resolved to interview more gently; while the pair weren't saints, they would have supplied information in due time if he'd just shown a little patience. He immediately forgot both resolutions when he drove through the Headquarters gate and saw that every front window was black.

Bamsan Kiet scrambled out of the Citroën and barged inside, fearing the worst of fears—the unknown. The central hallway was dark. His own office was dark. His dread eased somewhat at the sight of the main desk and the flickering reflection of a candle on the face of Sergeant Heng Fri, duty officer for the shift. Fri was an old hand, gaunt and wrinkled, Kiet's age and beyond. The intermittent yellow light was not complimentary. Fri looked as if he had just emerged from a casket.

"Two hours without electricity," Fri said with a sneer. "We're lucky it's a slow evening. One sneak thief with a mango and no place to hide it. A child. I lectured him and ordered him to work all day tomorrow for the produce peddler."

Fri's summary justice was effective in any environment, Kiet thought. In this lighting he must have appeared to the frightened young thief as a ghoul. "Has Metro said when our power will be restored?"

Fri said, "This is the rare occasion when they aren't to blame. I sent a man for an electrician. Who knows when he'll return with one?"

Kiet shrugged helplessly. "If it isn't Metro, it's the wiring. The French wired the building when you and I were soiling diapers, Fri."

"Hah," Fri snorted. "Our colonial masters are as innocent as Metro. I can tell you the cause, but you should hear it from him."

"Him?"

"Your prodigy," Fri said with a gap-toothed grin. "The boy wizard of criminal science."

"Captain Binh? Where?"

"The interrogation room."

Captain Binh and a uniform were there, the latter's arm upraised, pointing a flashlight beam at a table. Binh was hunched over it, operating on a machine with a screwdriver. The room smelled of burnt rubber.

Kiet allowed his eyes to adjust. The machine had rows of knobs, an arm cuff, a chest tube, and several wire electrodes. He recognized it as a polygraph, a lie detector, a gift from America. The device had been stored unused for lack of need and lack of qualified technicians, tropical humidity attacking its innards like bacteria. It shared quarters with a ballistics machine and a chemical spectrograph provided by the Russians, who were not about to be upstaged.

Binh looked up. "Superintendent, I plugged it in and *poof*. A short circuit from a loose wire, most likely. I'm sorry about the fuse box, but we did get to it with a fire extinguisher before the fire spread."

Kiet suppressed a groan. An honest and zealous error, he told himself. The loss of face in chastising Binh, of shaming him, would lead to days, if not weeks, of pouting. He didn't relish the prospect of pursuing McCloud's killer under the dead weight of an emotionally wounded adjutant.

"Yes, yes. All right. I assume you have a candidate for your truth extractor."

"I do. His name is Plaset Curj. He works for Lon Min as night customs supervisor."

"Why him?"

"His answers were the least satisfactory, Superintendent. He was afraid and arrogant and—" Binh said, rubbing thumb against fingers, "—Associate Deputy Minister Min shares the crumbs with everybody, yes, to keep them happy and silent, but this man, we've checked on him. He lives well. Very, very well."

"By least satisfactory answers, you mean what?"

"Total absence of answers. The others lied and attempted to evade in ridiculous ways. One fellow said he was sick and was in the latrine half the night. The tower operator claimed an intense workload; only two airplanes landed all night, Superintendent. On and on and so forth. Plaset Curj replied no to each question. He made no effort whatsoever to justify or elaborate."

"Under orders by Lon Min, or perhaps confident of Min's protection?"

Captain Binh nodded. "Exactly. And Curj is weak. If anybody breaks and gives us leads, it will be him. I believe he is the official that Min said he demoted, though Curj wouldn't admit it. If I were such a scapegoat, I'd want to be well paid for the humiliation."

"Shouldn't we invite him in for a chat?"

"I'd really prefer to have the polygraph in working condition first," Binh said. "I've been reading the manual that came with it. Did you know that they are 90% accurate with ordinary people and 67% accurate with sociopaths?"

"No," Kiet said. "I didn't."

50

"He's under surveillance, Superintendent. He's not going anywhere. Shouldn't we have every possible advantage?"

Kiet looked at the machine and its probes. Attach the tentacles to one ignorant of its function and a confession might be blurted out in terror. "Agreed."

"Tomorrow at the latest," Binh said, bending to the stricken gadget with his screwdriver. "I promise."

Kiet paused, considering whether or not to pull Binh aside and show him the rubies. Taking his closest aide into his confidence would be the right thing to do. But no. Splitting Binh's wild enthusiasm down a second fork would be silly at this point. Let him concentrate on plastering probes to Plaset Curj. The guilt Kiet felt for his decision was only a pinprick's worth.

He slipped outside to nightfall. At nineteen degrees north latitude, there was no twilight. The sun dropped as if a bucket had been thrown over it.

Kiet headed home, eager for sleep and the end to a long, long day. It was not to be.

9

TRUE, THE PROPERTY was walled, but definition of Bamsan Kiet's home as a "villa" was generous. Its builder and only prior owner was a tax administrator in the service of the last governor general. He was a Frenchman and middling bureaucrat with social ambitions, a pretentious fellow who believed he had created a miniature estate by surrounding himself with cement. The walls served a second function—alleviation of paranoia. At the time, the Viet Minh were taking their revolution to the cities of Indochina and the tax man feared—wrongly—that Hickorn colonials would also be victims of bombs and kidnappings.

The house itself was a modest four rooms, extremely comfortable by Luongan standards, but hardly an object of envy by the moneyed. So confining was the lot size that the two-meter stucco barriers and the wrought-iron spikes atop it cast continuous shadows on the courtyard and grounds. This was Kiet's sole objection to the place; absence of sunlight made growing plants on the grounds and in the rear courtyard impossible.

No sooner had the masonry dried than papers were signed in Geneva and the tax administrator was transferred home. Kiet bought the villa and lived in it with his beloved wife, Tien, until she perished in the cholera epidemic of 1966. He had lived there alone since.

Three times a week, a maid shopped, did laundry, and cleaned house. Two years ago, Kiet adopted a stray cat, an obese and arrogant animal of indeterminate age. The cat ate kitchen discards and came and went as it pleased. In the monsoons, it cried at the door like a baby and slept on its master's bed. During the dry season, it was seldom seen. Kiet punished the beast for its indifference by refusing to name it.

Kiet went in, unbuttoned his shirt, and walked straight to the refrigerator for a drink from a jug of boiled water. Though he was offended by Westerners' snide cracks about Hickorn's water system and believed the health officials who began disinfecting during the epidemic and certified it as safe henceforth, he had not taken a drink from a tap after Tien's death. Nor would he ever.

The jug was missing. Kiet cursed this day, each and every thing about it. He fumbled for the light switch.

"Bosha, no. Don't"

Kiet froze, startled by the voice, doubly startled by the use of his childhood diminutive. How many people addressed him as Bosha now? Few. His Royal Highness was one. He was too rattled to think of others. His mind drifted to Binh's residential security warnings and his New York dope junkies.

"Bosha, come here and sit, please. Join me. You're in no danger."

The voice was coming from behind him, from the dining table. Kiet turned and did what he was told. The voice was remotely familiar.

"Bosha, I apologize. I took your water. I was thirsty. Here."

The figure across from Kiet filled a glass and gave it to him. The figure then lighted a lantern. "This will be ample light. We can see to talk, but nobody can see inside. Breaking into your home, your unlocked home, was rude. Borrowing your water and locating this lantern in your cupboard was rude. I won't compound my rudeness by concealing my identity."

The lantern illuminated a smooth, amorphous face and wispy, black hair. The face had barely changed in twenty years. It belonged to the Chairman of the Central Committee of the Luongan Communist Party. Ril Thoi, leader of the Luong Rouge.

Kiet and Thoi were friends as children, had attended *lycée* together. On graduation, Kiet enlisted in the Hickorn Police Department. Ril Thoi studied law at the university and became an attorney. Thoi had relished politics for as long as Kiet could remember. He was a malcontent and a compulsive organizer.

In the early 1960s, Thoi's views turned so leftist that he was his own best law client. Kiet, as a police cadet, had been on a team that arrested Thoi at a noisy and destructive demonstration on the Luong University campus. Thoi spent four months in jail and Kiet risked his career and his freedom by sneaking extra food in for his friend. Following his release, Thoi fled to the highlands and formed the Luong Rouge.

"Twenty long years, Ril, and you look exactly the same. I'm envious."

Ril Thoi laughed. "You expected me to be shriveled. A goatee and a stooped back. Everybody pictures me as Ho Chi Minh."

"We couldn't know," Kiet said. "You haven't been photographed since your mug shot."

"My goal keeps me young, Bosha. Each morning that I awake is another step in my journey."

Kiet said nothing.

"You were apolitical as a boy. A born reactionary. Oh, how I wanted to shake some consciousness into you! Evidently you haven't altered your thinking."

"I enforce the law," Kiet said. "I would do so for any government that would have me. Communists prohibit murder and robbery too, don't they?"

"The people decide the laws in a just society, Bosha."

Here we go, Kiet thought. If he snapped at the bait, he'd be bombarded with dialectical materialism and class struggle, railed against as a paper tiger and an imperialist running dog. The Ril Thoi he knew could be as tedious in his own way as Ambassador Smithson. He shifted out of dogma into reality. "Aren't you taking a risk by coming to Hickorn?"

"I come to Hickorn whenever I please. I'm anonymous, Bosha. My following is in the countryside. The peasants. They are the heart of the revolution. Are you threatening me with arrest?"

"No. I'm alone and I imagine you have friends nearby. Our telephones function no better than they did when you took to the hills. If I ran to my phone for assistance, you'd be halfway to Obon before I got through to Headquarters."

"Thoi laughed again. "My pragmatic Bosha. This is just a reunion of two old friends, you know."

Kiet was dubious. "Yes, but allow me to make a comment outside of friendship. You say your revolution is in the countryside."

"For the present."

"For the extended present, please. If *plastique* begins blowing people out from under barstools, if automobiles explode, if foreign diplomats vanish—well, then I cease being apolitical. If you are planning to use 1960s Saigon as a model for—"

"Ho Chi Minh City."

"Saigon when the mischief was done, Ril. Hickorn is my city. I regard the safety of its citizens a personal responsibility."

"Believe me, I am just a visitor. I can't leave Hickorn soon enough. Its decadence sickens me. When the time is right, the revolution will sweep in and Hickorn will fall without a whimper.

"And you are my friend, Bosha. I can never forget our

boyhood, and your kindness when I was imprisoned. I wouldn't challenge you by ordering mischief, as you term it, not while you're burdened with the murder of an American adventurer. The killing oozes of corruption, doesn't it?''

So this was his objective, Kiet thought. Denny Mc-Cloud and his association with the Second Military District. "You too have burdens, Ril. Last week, nine of your guerrillas—''

"Revolutionary freedom fighters.''

"Yes, whatever. How did it happen? Your tactics are conservative and patient. I don't know your strength, but I doubt if you can easily afford the losses. General Vo's men are hardly aggressive. Did yours become careless?''

Kiet heard purring. Ril lifted the rotund cat from his lap and smiled. "I was waiting for you. He jumped up and fell asleep as if he'd known me all his life. I miss these simple domestic luxuries.''

Kiet knew he wasn't going to receive a direct answer. Ril Thoi always had been sly and circumlocutory. Conducting a conversation with him was like dancing with a partner on the other side of the room. He said, "Marsad Ref is a hero, you know. The American ambassador himself told me.''

The needling worked. Ril Thoi's tone hardened. "I have younger elements who are less conservative, less patient. They live for action. They can't grasp the concept of a class struggle. Old ideas give way slowly to new ideas. You cannot win with guns if the people do not yet have the heart to pick them up and fire them at their oppressors. And as you are aware, I do not have the necessary guns.''

Kiet resisted mentioning that Luongans under His Royal Highness were not oppressed. He didn't reply.

Ril continued, "Some of my men criticize my stubbornness, my refusal to accept aid from comrades outside of Luong. We are poorer than the poorest peasants. We need everything."

He paused and shook his head. "I could say the word and have anything I want, but I'd be betraying Luongan self-determination. I'd be in bed with Russians or Chinese or Vietnamese. They'd parachute advisors in and march me around like a puppet."

"I've never agreed with you," Kiet said, "but I've always admired your independence."

"As I've admired your integrity and efficiency as a police investigator. Politics is linear in comparison to a complex murder case."

"Bearing in mind that you are the government's ranking enemy and that I'm probably guilty of treason for speaking to you, what is it you would like to know about the Denny McCloud investigation?"

The cat was squirming in Ril Thoi's arms. He set it down. The animal ignored its master, jumped onto a counter and out an open window. "The ranking enemy. A high compliment."

"He usually purrs and rubs on my leg, begging for his supper. He doesn't declare me invisible until I feed him," Kiet said. "But you always have had a gift of persuasion."

"There was milk in the refrigerator," Thoi said with a sheepish grin.

"Regarding McCloud, please."

Ril Thoi's face tightened. "Your earlier reference to the heroic Colonel Ref. Seven of my nine men were killed in the firefight. The remaining two were disarmed and taken prisoner. Ref shot them, Bosha. His lackeys forced them to kneel and he shot them in the back of the head with his pistol. That won't be written in the narrative when he's decorated for bravery, but it's a fact. Marsad Ref, Chi Vo, and Dennis McCloud did business together.

They were inseparable when McCloud flew to Obon. In Hickorn, McCloud bought Ref's drinks and sluts."

"Your concern, then, is McCloud's conspiracy with Ref, not the apprehension of McCloud's murderer."

Thoi clasped his hands in front of him. "Is there a distinction? Opium and money was their bond. Money and opium made the murder inevitable."

"I'm exploring that theory," Kiet said.

Thoi laughed. "You're playing cagey, Bosha. One explores the unknown. McCloud terminated the partnership without Ref's knowledge. He swallowed a big loss exchanging zin with that slippery Indian, Singh."

"I should hire you as a detective, Ril. Perhaps you can further enlighten me and name McCloud's killer."

"Very simple. Vo and Ref were responsible, directly or indirectly. You don't wish to admit it, though, do you? How do you arrest a general and a chief of staff who command an army division, and survive to book them into your jail?"

"The crime occurred less than twenty-four hours ago," Kiet said coolly. "Of course the army men are candidates."

"Candidates to be arrested, tried in your courts, and executed, I presume. A hazardous task. I can help."

"How?"

"When you're ready to issue warrants, lure them to Hickorn on a pretense before making arrests. Nobody in the Hickorn garrison will do anything silly. If their loyalist troops in Obon decide to board airplanes and come to their aid, we'll divert their attention."

"Blow up airplanes, attack their headquarters?"

"Whatever has to be done."

Kiet said, "I sympathize. They ambushed nine of your men and, knowing Ref, I'll accept your story that he killed two in cold blood. But you're asking me to be party in starting a civil war. No."

Ril Thoi stood. He was wearing a suit and tie. His shoulders were rounded and his white shirt was baggy at the waist. He could have passed for a clerk in the Ministry of Agriculture. Kiet understood his mobility, how he blended into the populace. His mild appearance and demeanor also explained his popularity with the peasants, what popularity he enjoyed.

"Bosha, you're *preventing* a civil war. Reprisal is being discussed without my approval. My position since the incident is tenuous. Some of my youthful hotheads would willingly attack the army's Obon enclave and martyr themselves."

"White gloves off," Kiet said, nodding at the scenario. "General Vo and Colonel Ref assassinated by fanatic Marxist suicide squads. The fury of the Royal Luongan Army unleashed in retaliation."

"I'm not prepared for a full-scale conflict, Bosha. I never wanted one and never will. We *will* prevail, but through raised consciousness of the oppressed classes."

Ril Thoi the dreamer, Kiet thought. That was the secret to his youthfulness. One whose reality was a childlike fantasy could never grow old.

Kiet didn't question the zeal of Thoi's followers. He questioned their competence. He remembered an assault on a Second Military District fuel dump. It went amiss when the Rouge sapper became entangled in barbed wire protecting the outer perimeter and triggered his satchel charge.

"Luong benefits, therefore, if I'm the instrument of your vengeance."

"Yes."

"If they are guilty, they will be punished."

"I've told you they're guilty, Bosha. You know they're guilty."

"You've told me how you ache to have them found guilty."

59

"And you won't circumvent your stupid procedures and your outmoded concept of civil rights and arrest them immediately?"

"I'll circumvent my stupid procedures and my outmoded concept of civil rights," Kiet said, "when pigs can fly."

10

KIET DISMISSED RIL THOI'S story. A youthful faction of his barefoot Marxists on a blood vendetta? No, thank you. Kiet had never known a bona fide fanatic. He had read of them. The senile and homicidal mullahs of Iran, yes. That deranged Libyan too, grinning and shaking his fist at news cameras. The adolescents they encouraged to drive dynamite-laden trucks through barricades, to storm Western airliners with grenades and machine guns, certainly. These were holy warriors prodded by a God who had not graced Luong with His benevolence.

In Kiet's view, morbid fanaticism had been bred out of Luongans centuries ago. A torrid climate and an easy disposition rendered it a genetic impossibility. Even Ril Thoi's revolution moved at the pace of a Hickorn civil servant processing a visa application.

You acted recklessly only if there was something in it for you. Kiet could not visualize a rabid young Rouge throwing himself on barbed wire as a human ramp for a banzai charge by his comrades, all of whom would be cut down by Vo's praetorians. Sheer nonsense. Vengeance had narrower limits. It all came down to politics and business.

The envelope of rubies in Kiet's pocket burned his thigh. The prospect of a night's sleep was ridiculous. Maybe Ril Thoi knew about the damnable gems, but probably not. In any case, he was aching to learn why nine of his insurgents had gotten boxed in and slaughtered by government soldiers kilometers from any military objective. The rubies were the answer to an unknown question.

Kiet put on a fresh shirt and drove to the Yuppie's apartment. Susan's professed ignorance and naïveté was irritating him under the skin. She had slept with McCloud and loved him. Their intimacy must have transcended sticky bedsheets. Couldn't she have noticed a recent restlessness? Didn't he confide in her? Did he talk in his sleep? Anything.

Kiet's plan was to show her the rubies and say talk to me or else. He slowed at her building, but sped up at the sight of a lone car parked at the door. It was a black Simca with oxidized paint and diplomatic plates. Who from any embassy was out and about in a residential neighborhood at midnight? he wondered. No nightlife here. The tinny jazz bands and rock combos were downtown, at the Continental and the smart lounges. The only light on the block glowed yellow on Susan Dempsey-Mohn's curtains.

Kiet continued around the corner, went into the alley behind the apartment house, and used the rear entrance. Susan was coming down the main staircase. A short, pasty-complexioned man walked beside her. He wore a winkled brown suit, white shirt with a collar frayed by repeated washings, limp brown tie, a blank expression, and a bad haircut. Eyeglass lenses were thick and steel-framed. The man was to her left and his hand was stuffed into a bulging pocket. A Russian, Kiet thought. A Bolshevik in his sartorial splendor could be identified at fifty meters.

They descended in careful synchronization, the Soviet's pocket bulge grazing her hip. Susan glanced at Kiet, opened her mouth, but quickly closed it. She was obviously terrified.

Kiet walked up several steps, offered the man a coolie

smile, pressed against the railing, and gave him a hand wave to pass. The Russian nodded curtly, appreciative that the native knew his manners.

Kiet stooped to tie a shoelace. Susan and the Soviet stopped. "So solly," Kiet said in grinning pidgin. "Me buy cheapo shoe. They no stay tied."

Susan bit her lower lip and tensed her eyebrows. The Russian grunted. He nudged Susan and they continued downward. Faster. Kiet grabbed the Russian's ankle and raised up with all his might The Superintendent couldn't remember when he had last been agile, but age had stolen little of his considerable strength.

Susan lurched backward a step and clung to the opposite railing. Kiet had her companion's ankle with both hands now, arms vertical. He released him.

The Russian yelped and performed an inverted half pirouette. His hand came out of the bulging pocket for support. An automatic pistol clunked down to the lobby. He completed the maneuver with a double somersault and hit the floor flat on his back, spread-eagled.

His face was contorted in pain, but he was conscious and alert and uninjured. The pistol was just beyond his grasp. He rolled onto his side and reached for it. Susan arrived first and kicked. The gun bounced against the front door and came to rest by the mailboxes.

The Russian saw. He rose to his knees and crawled forward. Susan aimed another kick at his face, missed, and fell. Kiet, breathing heavily from exertion, was there. He landed on the Russian, rider to mount. The Russian collapsed under Kiet's weight and wheezed. He lay limply, his fight gone.

Susan scrambled for the pistol.

"Don't!" Kiet said.

She looked at him, eyes hot with adrenaline.

"Scuff it through the hallway with your foot. Out of range. don't touch it."

"Oh. For fingerprints?"

"Yes," he lied. The hammer was cocked. A careless caress of the trigger and justice could be perverted by an accidental hole through his own forehead. "Preservation of evidence."

Susan herded the steel cobra into the hall with mincing volleys. Kiet patted the clothing of the man beneath him. He found a handkerchief and a car key. No wallet, no papers. He wasn't surprised.

He got up, bringing the Russian up with him by his jacket collar. "Can we talk?"

Silence and a programmed stare. Kiet wanted very badly to slap him. But no. It would be like booting his cat.

"Go."

The Russian stared.

Kiet spun him around and shoved. "Go."

The Russian limped out the door.

Susan returned. "Where—"

"He escaped."

"Your gun?"

Kiet shrugged. "I don't carry a weapon. The shoulder strap chafes and gives me rashes."

"Jesus," she moaned. "I don't believe any of this."

"And I would be creating an international incident. The day is alive with them."

"You can't just let him escape after he tried to kidnap me," she protested.

"I can and I did," he said, pointing upward. "To your apartment, please. We'll talk."

11

"YOU *KNOW* HIM?"

"Unfortunately I do," Susan told Kiet. "His name is Sergei Pudkin and he's attached to the Soviet Embassy."

Kiet sipped the beer Susan had given him. It was an American-brewed "light." The amber color was proper, but it tasted to him like Golden Tiger that had been strained through charcoal and cheesecloth, then wrung from a sponge. "I guessed by his impeccable tailoring that he was Russian."

Susan laughed. "His title is Scientific and Engineering Attaché. I don't know what he really does except act as a gofer for Ambassador Kalashnikov."

Scientific and Engineering Attaché easily translated into KGB—a technician in charge of spy electronics, all that metal bristling on the embassy roof. But gopher? The reference to a burrowing North American rodent perplexed him. If he was ever to totally communicate with this woman, he would be forced to enroll in a Berlitz refresher. "You were in the process of being kidnapped by a man you were acquainted with?"

"Acquainted with, yes. Nothing further. He's a pest and a nerd. He was Kalashnikov's intermediary, his— John Alden."

"Excuse me?"

"Myles Standish used John Alden to court Priscilla Mullens by remote control in the days of the Pilgrims. It was a famous Longfellow poem they say is fictional, but

I'd like to think not. Anyway, it backfired and Priscilla married John. Never mind. I'm so hyper, I'm running off at the mouth."

Nerd? Hyper? Kiet gulped his beer and asked for another. She brought it and he said, "I'm thoroughly confused, but I'm catching romance somewhere in your explanation."

She sighed and shook her head furiously. Long soft hair swung half a cycle behind the motion. "A crazy, kinky kind of romance I definitely didn't encourage. I've never met Ambassador Kalashnikov. I wouldn't know him from the man in the moon.

"He's seen me, but I haven't a clue when or where. He developed this weird fixation and started sending Pudkin here with gifts and invitations for me to visit him at his embassy."

"What gifts?"

"You're drinking one. Jazz records too. Old Gerry Mulligan 78s I bet came from his own collection. Blue jeans, a Walkman, quarts of Coca-Cola in glass bottles, and a sack of potatoes," she said, ticking them off on her fingers.

"Commodities highly treasured in their society," Kiet said. "If I'm to believe what I've heard, consumer goods are in short supply. People in Moscow stand in line to buy shoe polish and oranges. Very flattering."

"Flattering maybe, welcomed no. Lately, it's been costume jewely, candy, lingerie, and dirty books. Really gross stuff. The text was in Cyrillic, which I don't read, thank God, and the pictures were fuzzy black-and-whites of—well, you can imagine. I thought pornography was illegal in Russia."

"You didn't return his overtures, even to dispatch a note with Pudkin saying that you weren't interested?"

"No way. And I haven't bothered to be polite lately.

It's gone on since a week after I moved into this apartment, before and after Dennis came into my life."

"Could it have been a harmless encounter at a social function? You were introduced. You immediately forgot. He didn't. He was struck by your beauty and subsequently obsessed by it."

Susan blushed through her tan. "I don't do the cocktail-party circuit. I'm positive I've never seen Ambassador Kalashnikov face-to-face."

Kiet was skeptical. "The foreign community in Hickorn is small. Less than two thousand Americans and Europeans. You are an attractive, outgoing person."

"My research keeps me from the party crowd, Superintendent," she said, a flash of anger in her voice. "I'm here to study Luong and its people, not the parasites who spend money on *Lé Avenue*. You're insinuating that I'm being less than candid with you and I resent it."

"Unintentionally less than open," Kiet said, raising his hands in mock surrender.

"Oh, I've seen his photograph in the Hickorn *Post*. I read it every day with my dictionary and grammar books to teach myself written Luongan. They had an article on him. He looks like a linebacker who's gone to seed. His wife and teenaged sons are in Leningrad. His rationale for leaving them home is that the boys are preparing for Red Army officer training. The dedicated family man. Fat chance. He's a middle-aged lecher sowing his oats without interference."

Kiet pondered: If Sergei Pudkin is a nerd and Ambassador Kalashnikov is a linebacker, what is my status if this woman anoints me with a strange noun? "How did Denny McCloud react to this attention?"

"He thought it was funny. He answered the knock one night. Pudkin was standing there holding a box of Czechoslovakian chocolates. Dennis towered over him. I thought Pudkin was going to have a stroke. They argued.

Dennis spoke in Russian. I don't know what he said, but Pudkin turned white as a sheet. Dennis took the chocolates and slammed the door in his face. He refused to repeat the conversation. He just said that he put a dumb Russki in his place."

"Cruel," Kiet said. "The man was merely doing a distasteful chore for his superior."

"Dennis had a mean streak in him," Susan agreed. "I didn't see it often. I wouldn't have fallen for him if I had. As happy as I was that he got rid of Pudkin, we got into a fight over his method. Dennis reverted to his little-boy mode and said he was sorry. He told me he was big for his age as a child, all through school. He played football and made all-state. If the chance arose to show off, the bully in him couldn't quite die, though he really wanted it to. Thinking about it now, Dennis really knew how to push my buttons."

"Pudkin played the faithful lackey. Tonight he progressed from your folklore Alden character to kidnapper. No candies or Levis."

"That gun's still downstairs," she said, suddenly remembering.

"Unimportant."

"But you said it should be preserved for evidence."

"I'll retrieve it on the way out. More germane is Sergei Pudkin's bearing a nine-millimeter Browning instead of a bouquet. What transpired?

"He came to the door and said that Ambassador Kalashnikov desired my company and would I please join him for tea and cake. That was pretty much the usual pitch. Well, in my frame of mind, I wasn't ready to deal with it. I tried to close the door, but he pushed his way in and stuck the gun in my face. No pleading and no charming persuasion for a change. He said to *go*. Your timing was beautiful, Superintendent Kiet."

"I have a theory. I can perhaps explain Ambassador Kalashnikov's ardor."

"I would appreciate that very much."

"I'll answer your question, then I hope you will answer some of mine."

Susan tightened, on guard. "I already—well, sure."

"Come, please," Kiet said, taking her to the roof of the building. "What do you see?"

She handled the question as if it were a grenade. "It's a lovely night. The stars. Hickorn would be an astronomy student's paradise."

"No, I meant lower, Hickorn's skyline."

"Lovely too. At this hour you see a light here and there, scattered, like starlight. People in Hickorn retire early. Is that your point? I'm not catching the gist of this."

"The Soviet Embassy is pitch-black, but I don't believe for an instant that they retire early," Kiet said patiently. "See how it dominates even at night? It blocks the downtown glitter. If there were a full moon low in the sky behind it, the monstrosity would bathe us in shadows."

"The place is creepy. Those tiny windows are dark any time of the night or day."

"One-way glass," Kiet said. "They can see out, you can't see in."

"So?"

The embarrassed Kiet struggled for words. His revelation would take him past the bounds of both police investigator and gentleman. Better he coax the answer from her own lips. "Your tanned complexion results from lying up here in midday, does it not?"

She looked at him. "How did you know?"

"Hearsay reports, I assure you."

"From whom?"

"Irrelevant. Hickorn merchants who sell optical

equipment say that East German binoculars are among the finest in the world."

Susan stared at the embassy, an alternative to facing Kiet. "I feel like a complete idiot, but thanks anyway. Wow! The number-one Russian in Luong is a Peeping Tom. He just had to have what I so stupidly let him feast his beady little eyes on."

Kiet also gazed at the concrete beast that concealed everything within. He knew Kalashnikov and couldn't argue with Susan's description of him and her conclusions. His office was on a top-floor corner, one or more windows facing this direction. He visualized the Russian at siesta time, seeking stimulation when most of Hickorn was dozing to avoid it, aiming his high-quality binoculars at Susan with one hand, manipulating something else with the other.

The here and now was bothering him. It wasn't inconceivable that they were being observed via some sort of infrared spyglass apparatus.

Ril Thoi in town to hold an innocent reunion with his old chum Bosha. The science attaché, Sergei Pudkin, brandishing a firearm. The scene didn't calculate. Throw in Kalashnikov, and Kiet pictured three noses smudging Eastern Bloc glass, he and Susan the object of their peep show.

He took her arm, to lead her downstairs. It was trembling, elbow tight to her side, fingers webbed over her face. Kiet released her and waited, ashamed at his morose self-pity for how his own day had gone. This woman had lost her lover, had nearly been kidnapped, and had been ogled in the nude for an interminable period without her permission or knowledge by a Marxist voyeur. Kiet touched his chest. His heart beat. He was grateful.

Finally she said, "I'm okay. We can go."

In Susan's apartment, Kiet placed the rubies carefully in her hand.

Her eyes widened and her mouth fell open. "Are they what I think they are?"

"If my information is correct, they come from the Mogok Valley in Upper Burma. They're nicknamed pigeon bloods for their wonderful color. Only rubies of this origin are so honored."

Susan seemed hypnotized by them. "They must be worth a fortune."

Kiet looked at her closely and said, "They are. Have you ever seen them before?"

Her eyes registered genuine surprise. "No. Why do you think I would've?"

"They were found in Mr. McCloud's, uh, possession."

"On his body?"

"Essentially yes. Now, while I truly hate to bruise your emotions further, I have to ask for more frankness on your part regarding Mr. McCloud's business dealings."

"I've already said that he flew passengers and freight and had a government contract. He kept his professional life separate from our relationship."

"Susan, I'm not disputing that he was secretive to you about his work. I'm asking for indirect observations, speculations."

"Such as?"

Kiet sighed. She was compelling him to dig it out of her in fragments. "His income, please. Money and how he spent it."

"I know he made a good living. He always carried a large wad of zin when we went out. We ate and drank very well. He tried to pay my rent. I refused and that angered him. I have enough to get by on and I didn't want to feel like he was keeping me, *especially* since he refused to live with me."

"Any signs of financial difficulties?"

"Well, possibly. We'd be at the Continental and he'd receive long-distance phone calls. He'd come back from the phone in a foul mood. I'd ask and he'd make a crack about buzzards. On a couple of occasions, shopkeepers approached him while we were on the *terrasse*. Dennis and the men talked in private for a few minutes. I couldn't overhear, but Dennis smiled a lot and talked fast. He'd return none too happy."

"Creditors?"

Susan shook her head. "I learned fast that bugging him was futile. He'd clam up and the evening would be ruined."

Insects and shellfish? English was a maddening language of colloquialisms. A century of conversing with natives from their Los Angeles Lotusland and dead spots in his fluency would still remain. "McCloud appeared to be departing Luong permanently when he was murdered."

She glanced at her lap. "I can't admit that to myself yet."

"The rubies were contraband," Kiet said gently. "Mr. McCloud was smuggling them out of the country."

"If you say so, but my research has revealed nothing about black-market jewels."

"Nor has mine," Kiet said. "Opium is Luong's shadow industry."

"I know. It's even spelled out in some Luong guidebooks."

Kiet paused. He expected either denial or tears, but Susan's expression was level, her reply matter-of-fact. "I'm not as gullible as I let on, Superintendent. Dennis's Second Military District clients aren't lily white."

"And Dennis himself?"

"He reminded me of a Wild West prospector. He was capable of gambling on a big score. That was the child in him. But opium? God, I loved the man! I'm not prepared to despise his memory."

Kiet, the detective, recalled Dr. Pho's description of her visit, her anxious request for McCloud's cremation. Kiet, the lay psychologist, thought: incinerate the flesh, incinerate any vestige of evil into hot vapors. Nothing survies but ashes and unsoiled remembrances.

Kiet reclaimed the rubies and said, "Prior to Copernicus and Galileo, the Earth was the center of the universe. These stones are a parallel. Hickorn orbits them."

Susan understood. "Sergei Pudkin. You're saying that the Russians are interested in the rubies and think I have them?"

Kiet nodded. "For what reason, I don't know, but if you had been taken to the Soviet Embassy at gunpoint in the middle of the night, you would not have—"

"Ever seen the light of day again," Susan finished. "Your jailing Sergei Pudkin would be a tame international incident compared to what I'd've created by blabbing to our embassy, the media, and anybody else who would listen."

"I'm placing you under round-the-clock security," Kiet said.

"At your headquarters?"

"No. My jail is for criminals. Amenities are few. That would be unfair. Tonight here, if I may sleep on your sofa. Tomorrow, my home. There is more room, and I'll post guards."

"I'd rather not be confined, like I'm under house arrest. If I can't continue my work, I'll go bananas."

"Agreed. My officers will accompany you while you're out researching."

"I pride myself as being so independent, I'm sometimes obnoxious on the subject," Susan said. "But under these circumstances, no argument. Do me one favor, though."

"Yes?"

"Please bring up Pudkin's gun."

Kiet did. When he returned to the apartment, Susan had fitted the sofa with a sheet and provided a pillow. "Sweet dreams."

Kiet placed the pistol under the pillow, stretched out, and kicked off his shoes. Susan covered him with a second sheet.

"Gautama Buddha," she said. "You kind of remind me of him."

Kiet did not hear her. He was already snoring.

12

IN THE MORNING Bamsan Kiet installed Susan Dempsey-
Mohn in his spare bedroom. He apologized for the dust
and said that the housekeeper would be in later. Susan
said nonsense and asked where brooms and mops were
kept. Kiet had to think for a moment, but did locate
them. He then telephoned Binh and asked him to come
over immediately with two uniformed officers.

When Binh arrived, Susan was in shorts and tee shirt,
sweeping cat-sized dust kittens from beneath the bed,
complaining that a product called Lemon Pledge was
unavailable in Hickorn.

Kiet made brief introductions, describing Susan as a
"material witness in protective custody" in a tone that
erased the young adjutant's leer. He ordered the uniforms to stay with her at all times and to be alert for
danger. He handed them the keys to the Citroën and told
them to take Mrs. Dempsey-Mohn wherever she wanted,
as long as it was within the city limits.

Binh and Kiet drove to Headquarters in an old Renault
Dauphine. That and the Citroën were the only Hickorn
Police Department cars not assigned on patrol, and the
decrepit Renault shimmied at any speed and had a ten-
dency to pop out of gear. Binh pouted all the way and
Kiet knew it was because he was being silently accused
of trading the Citroën for sexual favors.

The silence was welcomed. Kiet's head and back hurt
from the lumpy couch, and his shoulders were sore from

hoisting Sergei Pudkin. He was in no humor for exuberant chatter about polygraphs and police science.

In his office, Kiet showed Binh the rubies and recounted yesterday's affairs. Binh absorbed the news in quiet awe and said, "Superintendent, you are aware of what I was thinking and I'm sorry."

Kiet waved a hand. "Never mind. She's an attractive young lady. To be considered capable of seducing her is a compliment. Your suggestion of an autopsy, by the way, was brilliant. Without it, there would be no rubies. We would be chasing our tails in pursuit of my worthless opium theories."

Captain Binh beamed. "Thank you, but where is our investigation headed? My informants have never uttered the word ruby, but apparently even the communists are mixed up in them."

Kiet shrugged—slowly, in deference to his aching shoulders. "We merely have extra puzzle pieces to gather, Captain. What do you have to report?"

"I've taken Plaset Curj into custody," Binh said.

"Your lie detector machine is repaired?"

"I'm afraid it isn't, Superintendent. The electronics inside the case are roasted. The instructions say that replacement parts are to be purchased from the factory in Chicago, although a sticker on the chassis says that it was assembled in Hong Kong. An indefinite delay, I figured. We arrested Curj as he was coming off work at the airport this morning."

"A wise decision," Kiet said. "Has Mr. Curj relieved his conscience?"

"No, Superintendent. He just sits like a stone. I've left him alone with his thoughts in the interrogation room."

"Good," Kiet said, rising awkwardly. "Shall we?"

The interrogation room smelled of perspiration and last night's electrical fiasco. The room was windowless and painted a purposely depressing gray. It was furnished with a table, padded swivel chairs for the interviewers, and a metal stool for the subject. Dangling over the table was a bare light, the brightest incandescent bulb sold in Hickorn. Bamsan Kiet had been the interior decorator. Kiet prohibited physical abuse of prisoners, but had no objection if the atmosphere raised false anxieties in that regard.

The man on the stool was slouched and sullen. He was in his twenties, handsome and longhaired. Kiet noticed manicured fingernails. A dandy, he thought. Lon Min's protégé.

"He's wearing Italian shoes, Superintendent," Binh said.

"Is that a silk shirt, Mr. Curj?" Kiet asked.

Plaset Curj acknowledged the policemen by lifting his head slightly and addressing the table with a smirk.

"Oh, he has shrewd secrets," Kiet said, angered by Curj's smug contempt.

"He also has a brand-new Honda motorbike," Binh said. "His lady friends ride to the Continental *terrasse* on the back of it. They eat shrimp and drink cognac and dance to disco records."

"Ah," Kiet said at the reminder of the Ma San River crustaceans.

"*French* cognac," Binh said. "Vintages that have dust on the bottle."

"I can afford only Golden Tiger with the delicacy," Kiet said, sighing.

"Curj's salary as night customs supervisor was thirty thousand zin per month, Superintendent. His demotion reduced him to twenty-four thousand."

Kiet calculated in his notebook. "Forty U.S. dollars a month. At LaCroix's prices, that would cover cocktails and appetizer. I envy your budgeting skills, Mr. Curj."

"Answer the superintendent," Binh snapped.

No visible response.

"Might I talk to Mr. Curj alone, Captain?"

Binh rolled his eyes and left, saying, "All you'll hear is your own voice."

Kiet took one of the chairs, leaned forward so his face was at the same level as the slouching airport employee's, rested his chin on folded arms, and stared.

Five minutes of this and Plaset Curj was completely unnerved. "Stop it!" he blurted. "Stop your games! I don't have to say anything unless my lawyer is present."

Kiet groaned and buried his head. So this was the problem. Binh had been at it again, reading to suspects from a little card he carried in his wallet, something given him by his District of Columbia police mentors. It was called a Miranda warnings card.

Kiet stood up suddenly and slammed his palms on the table. His chair shot backward on its casters, struck the wall, and tipped over. "Listen to me," he shouted. "You are the victim of a misunderstanding. You do not have the right to remain silent. As far as I'm concerned, your silence is admission of guilt. If you retain these silly notions, they will be reported to your judge."

Curj's posture had improved. "My—judge?"

"You aren't a deaf mute. Splendid. Your judge, yes, at your trial. You are implicated in a murder. If the killers are not brought to justice, you will stand charges of conspiracy, be found guilty, and shot."

"You're bluffing me."

Kiet wasn't, not entirely. "Wake up, man! This is Luong, not the United Nations."

"But am I not entitled to a lawyer?" Curj replied in a whisper.

"Luongan law has no patience with slippery technicalities. Your defense is truth and innocence. If those qualities are lacking, the smoothest shyster in the world can't prevent you from being blindfolded against sandbags."

"Sir, I didn't kill the American pilot," Curj said weakly.

"To conspire is to act in harmony," Kiet said. "You need not touch the knife. Now tell me, did you see Mr. McCloud the day before yesterday?"

Curj hesitated, then said, "Yes, sir. He flew soldiers in from Obon. He filed a flight plan for Bangkok. I approved his manifest."

"The phantom thousand kilos of rice?"

"I was instructed to sign the papers, sir."

"Without a physical inspection?"

"Yes, sir. I am normally conscientious. I was following orders."

"There was no cargo of any kind on his Caribou."

"Yes, sir. I know. An out-of-country flight in an empty aircraft arouses suspicions."

"A routine freight shipment was the desired impression?"

"Yes, sir."

"Upon whose orders?"

"Lon Min's."

Resentment sharpened the delicate lines of Curj's face. Kiet said, "Associate Deputy Minister Min blamed you for failing to notice McCloud's airplane on the apron all night despite an eight P.M. takeoff time, and reduced you in rank. In my opinion, his action was highly unfair."

Kiet hoped for an explosion of grievances. Instead, Curj said without emotion, "Somebody has to be accountable, sir. A man in Lon Min's position cannot lose face. As you have said, this is Luong."

"What, please, is the source of your supplementary income? Be free to elaborate, Mr. Curj. I seek vicious killers. I'm not concerned with ingrained corruption."

"My inspection of baggage and cargo can be conveniently incomplete, sir."

"In your haste, you occasionally overlook questionable belongings and freight packages? Pliable grayish substances, for instance?"

"Yes, sir. Opium gum."

"And what other forms of contraband, please?"

"Birds, sir. Once only."

"Excuse me?"

"A year ago, a Dutchman who owned pet shops smuggled a planeload of birds. Thousands of tiny, wild Luongan birds. Protected species. In cages. On a DC-10 widebody."

Kiet closed his eyes, staggered by the venality of Luong's customs officials. "Opium. Birds. The Royal Palace next, stone by stone, for exhibition in a California amusement park. What else?"

"Nothing that I have been directly associated with, sir."

The denial sounded genuine. "Is Associate Deputy Minister Min compensating you for the humiliation and reduction in rank?"

"He promises to be generous, sir, if I'm discreet and I obey him."

"The soldiers McCloud ferried in from Obon, did you recognize any of them? I've been informed that the passenger manifest was accidentally lost."

"Not accidentally, sir. Lon Min sent me to the office to do paperwork while he supervised the floor. He ordered me to destroy the manifest. And my customs inspectors were told by Min not to leave the terminal. Anything besides the suitcases of incoming and outgoing passengers on commercial flights was not their business that night."

While Lon Min was allegedly off duty, Kiet thought. "Were McCloud and Min together, to your knowledge?"

"They had a brief conference in Min's private office shortly after McCloud landed from Obon, sir."

"A very important question, Mr. Curj. Do you remember who McCloud brought in on the Obon run?"

"Soldiers. The majority were enlisted men. Their names weren't familiar to me."

"Officers?"

Plaset Curj gulped and daintily dabbed his sweating forehead with a handkerchief.

"Out with it, man," Kiet coaxed. "You have been doing wonderfully."

"We are speaking in confidence, sir?"

"Absolutely."

"Lieutenant Colonel Marsad Ref. I don't like him, sir. If he knew I mentioned his name—"

"He won't," Kiet broke in. "Did you actually see him?"

"I didn't, sir. Honestly I didn't."

"We're finished, Mr. Curj. I thank you for your candor."

"Wait—sir, when am I going to be released?"

"By and by," Kiet said, hurrying out.

Binh was waiting with an I-told-you-so look. Kiet told him what Curj had said. "I'd estimate he confessed roughly fifty percent of what he really knows. He may have been an eyewitness, but he's too afraid of dying to say more."

"Superintendent, how did you—"

"You deserve much of the credit, Captain. You softened Mr. Curj up for me. It is like what happens when one attempts to unscrew a jar. One tries and tries until one's face is purple. One yields it to a second party who opens it easily because of the tension applied by the first party."

The parable seemed to soothe Binh's ego. "Shall we hold him or turn him loose?"

Kiet thought for a moment. "Keeping him as our guest for several days would be wise for two reasons. Lon Min and Marsad Ref surely know we have him in custody. Curj will be safe here."

"The second reason," said a smiling Binh, "is Min's and Ref's apprehension at what Curj has confessed. I doubt that Ref would panic and do anything foolish, but Lon Min might. If we're lucky, we'll be flushing a game bird from the bush."

"Excellent," Kiet said.

"Twenty-four-hour surveillance on Min?" Binh asked.

"Please supervise the operation yourself."

"And your next move, Superintendent?"

"I have several possibilities," Kiet said. "I'll undertake the least pleasant first."

13

BAMSAN KIET WOULD not admit to fear of flying any more than he would admit that the sight of blood and torn flesh turned his stomach upside down and his knees into jelly. In fact, flying and murdered bodies affected him quite similarly.

Royal Air Luong's Hickorn-Obon shuttle aggravated the condition. The shuttle airplane was a Douglas DC-3, a loud and vibrating twin-engine craft whose manufacture coincided with Kiet's birth. Every seat was occupied on this run, baggage and infants nestled on the laps of the passengers. Lashed down in the aisle was cargo ranging from caged chickens to truck carburetors. The entry door had been permanently removed to facilitate loading and unloading. Kiet did not find the breeze refreshing.

Hickorn's Superintendent of Police was the flight's most important person. Out of respect, he had been assigned a forward seat. Whenever the lone attendant passed—a gap-toothed woman with the stocky legs and arms required to off-load truck carburetors—Kiet smiled appreciatively, turned toward the window, and pretended to drink in the view. Actually, his eyes were shut. A spectacular loss of face was at risk here.

He knew what was below anyway, so far below: neat checkerboards of rice paddy and verdant forest scratched by a winding gray ribbon—the Hickorn-Obon highway; beyond, to the north, hard green bumps on the planet—mountains spiked with hardwood timber and valleys where opium poppies flourished. Foreign aid had subsidized the 175 kilometers of asphalt and clay but it could not be traveled except in armed convoys because of the Rouge and their land mines and their sniping. Kiet silently cursed Ril Thoi.

After a long, long hour in the air, the plane thumped onto gravel and sod and taxied to the terminal. Obon was, in effect, capital of Luong's highlands. It was dusty and hilly and ramshackled, a mirror of the region's subsistence agriculture and mining, not urban by any stretch of the definition. Its airport terminal was consistent with the poverty and isolation. Kiet read *National Geographic;* the structure reminded him of a barn in an article on an American grain province named Nebraska.

Distrusting the ability of Hickorn's telephones to connect with Obon, let alone across the street, Kiet had radioed Second Military District Headquarters on a shortwave abandoned by the French. Despite static and oppressive heat radiated by vacuum tubes, Kiet got through and, yes, Brigadier General Chi Vo would be delighted to see him, would find time in his hectic schedule to accommodate the visit.

A jeep with a silver star set in a red bumper placard awaited him on the ramp. Kiet disembarked on wobbly legs and walked to it. Behind the wheel was Lieutenant Colonel Marsad Ref, beside him Brigadier General Vo.

"Kiet, it's nice to see someone from Hickorn," said General Vo, who was smiling but not offering a handshake. "I received your message and rejoiced. Life in the highlands is lonesome and austere. Hickorn deskpounders avoid our inconveniences. If my mission wasn't so vital, I'd lobby His Royal Highness for reassignment to soft duty in the Capital Military District."

Austere, Kiet thought? Chi Vo was as round as he was tall. He had the scruffy, oily look of the opium warlords he was pledged to combat. All he lacked to complete the image was chin whiskers and bandoliers.

Marsad Ref, on the other hand, was a recruiting poster. His camouflage fatigues were starched like cardboard, trouser creases sharp enough to slice the toughest cut of water buffalo. He wore a leather pistol belt and twin Colt .45 automatics, each nickel-plated and highly polished. Under his cap with its two lieutenant colonel's pips was a shaven reptilian head. Ref's hands remained on the steering wheel. Any reaction to Kiet's presence was concealed behind mirrored sunglasses.

"I am grateful for your time, sir. I wouldn't bother you unless the matter was urgent," Kiet said, measuring his words. He outlined the McCloud murder, withholding mention of the pigeon blood rubies.

"I heard sketchy details," Vo said, shaking his head. "Terrible. I knew McCloud well. For an American, he wasn't a bad man. His flying for us was dependable. That Caribou of his was a flying piece of junk, but he kept it patched together and held to the schedules he promised."

"He recently fitted it with long-range fuel tanks," Kiet said.

"If you say so. Aviation is too technical for me, Kiet. I'm a soldier, not an engineer."

"Circumstances lead me to believe that Mr. McCloud was trying to leave Luong for good when he was killed."

"You're a renowned detective, Kiet," Vo said, a trace of mockery in his voice. "I trust your conclusions."

"General, did you happen to see him the day before yesterday? His final charter was from here to Hickorn with soldiers," Kiet said, glancing at Marsad Ref.

Ref showed no emotion, but the question erased much of the congeniality from Vo's face. "I don't remember. My troops and I can barely hold the opium bandits and the Rouge at bay. I cannot be troubled to monitor the activities of a mercenary pilot. You aren't interrogating me, are you, Kiet?"

Collaboration with the opium bandits and indifference toward the Rouge is more accurate, Kiet thought. "Oh no, General. I have the utmost respect for the manner in which you are fighting Luong's enemies, and for your intelligence-gathering capabilities. The latter explains my purpose. I'm hoping that you have chanced upon information useful in my investigation. By the way, congratulations are in order for your victory last week against the Rouge, especially to you, Colonel Ref. If you aren't decorated by His Royal Highness himself, the world is unjust."

Marsad Ref raised a finger from the steering wheel and nodded.

"I'll check with my men for clues, Kiet," Vo said. "I have no firm knowledge of McCloud's dealing in opium, but that's what it may be centered on. If so, McCloud disappoints me. He betrayed my faith in him by smuggling. I noticed no criminal inclinations and I ate and drank and enjoyed camaraderie with the man. He was a hearty and likable fellow."

"The soldiers who were on the flight, they could perhaps help."

"They're relaxing in Hickorn and I envy them," Vo said. "Go home and ask them in person."

"I do not have their names, General. The passenger manifest was mysteriously lost. Perhaps your people have records."

"I'll consult my clerks," Vo said. "They'll get to it when they can, but who knows when that will be. Second District is tossed the scraps. I'm always understaffed."

Translation: never. "None of the troops have returned to Obon?"

"No. Leaves and transfers, probably. No courier was

dispatched that day. Enlisted men have it over generals. Indispensability is a curse, Kiet."

"There were no officers on the run?"

"Ref?"

Marsad Ref shook his head no.

"My chief of staff is on top of everything concerning our officers, Kiet. Sorry."

"Opium came to mind instantly," Kiet said. "None was found in the search of the plane, McCloud's body, or his room at the Continental."

Chi Vo laughed. "They killed him and took it. If that's not apparent to you, I should have your job."

"Opium is logical, except for one thing."

"Which is?"

"Telegrams to him from a Bangkok gem dealer. His mail slot at the Continental desk is stuffed with them," Kiet lied. "I called the gem dealer this morning and he'd divulge nothing. He said it was a private business affair. By gems, do we mean diamonds or do we mean star sapphires or emeralds or what? The scoundrel wouldn't elaborate."

"Strange," General Vo said evenly. "You could excavate Luong soil until you broke out in Mexico and you wouldn't find a crystal of cloudy quartz."

"The telegrams were terse. They begged for the next shipment."

"Are you suggesting that McCloud was illegally trafficking in gemstones?"

"Only the possibility, sir. If Luong is the highway for a new form of smuggling, I thought your men might have heard rumors. If not, I hope my speculation will be of use to you."

"I'm grateful, Kiet. We'll be on the alert for black-market jewels, but I'd advise you to concentrate on opium. I'm guessing that McCloud and the Bangkok dealer were doing perfectly legitimate business. Opium, Kiet. Opium will lead you to your killer."

"I will follow your suggestion, sir. Thank you."

Vo looked at Kiet and pointed to the DC-3 shuttle. "Kiet, they've refueled. If you rush, you can catch the turnaround flight to Hickorn. How I'd love to be on it."

So this was the extent of Vo's hospitality, Kiet thought. No luncheon, no drinks, no propaganda tour of counterinsurgency and drug interdiction operations.

"Inform me of progress on your case, will you?" Vo added. "McCloud and I had fond experiences. I'll drink a few whiskeys to him and savor our friendship. Damn his soul to hell if he was profiteering, but he was nevertheless an enjoyable character."

"I will, sir."

"Have a safe flight, Kiet."

"I will, sir. And you have a nice day."

14

TIRES KISSED THE Hickorn runway hard. The DC-3 had a change of heart and ballooned. But gravity objected, winning its argument halfway down. The starboard tire touched, then the port. Finally, the tailwheel thudded onto pavement and stuck. Brakes squealed with the noise of an orchestra of out-of-tune violins. The antique plane stopped one hundred meters from the end of the strip.

Kiet's hands gripped his knees like barnacles. He flexed whitened fingers and thanked whichever deity responsible for not yanking the sky out from under him, for pronouncing that he should live another day. He drove to Headquarters through a bouquet scent of taxicab and motorized pedicab and private automobile and city bus and military truck fumes, through wild and diagonal and wrong-way traffic that seemed positively benign in comparison to air travel.

Binh was signed out, shadowing Lon Min. Sergeant Heng Fri was on the desk, browbeating and cajoling policemen and citizens alike. The human element under Fri's control, Kiet closed his office door and attended to the minutiae of Hickorn police work.

A gun permit application submitted by a Japanese diplomat. A vague fear of international terrorist kidnappings and assassinations stated on the narrative. Kiet wished foreign guests would cancel delivery of their home newspapers, would cut the cables of Teletypes clattering inside their embassies, would forget the outside world. Hickorn was not Beirut. The application had been forwarded by a consular official in the Foreign Ministry, a note attached requesting priority handling. Thus a bribe had been paid. Though Hickorn had no gun-control regulations, Kiet initialed the document and tossed it in his out box. If there was no harm, everyone should be happy and content.

A shift change request, a patrolman petitioning transfer from nights to days, the officer pleading defective night vision. A paperclipped confidential note from Heng Fri saying the man's eyes were 20–20, but that he suspected his wife of infidelity. Kiet forgave the fib and reassigned the man to administrative duty. There were ample armed cuckolds on Hickorn's streets without his department contributing to their number.

A knock. Kiet yelled come in. One of the officers he had posted at his home entered and stood stiffly. "Superintendent, the telephones were out of order," he said nervously.

"They usually are in the afternoon," Kiet said, containing himself. "You've deserted your station to tell me that our phone system is unreliable?"

The officer gave Kiet an envelope. "She insisted, Superintendent. I didn't want to. My partner is at your house. The lady is safe, I swear to you."

A blushing Kiet waved him out, saying, "Yes, yes, I understand. Good. I'll see you later."

He opened the envelope and read: Didn't do diddly exc go shopping and to the mortuary, said goodbye to Dennis, cremation set for Wednesday if you okay, am occupying myself with special dinner to say thanks, can you be here sixish? you can't, pls inform. S.

Kiet reread it, referring to an English grammar handbook. Chapters on punctuation and abbreviations confused him further. He ignored the odd syntax and satisfied himself with a superficial understanding of the message. But he couldn't penetrate the "sixish." What language would glue suffixes onto numbers and why?

Captain Binh walked in.

"Ah, how is our friend, Associate Deputy Minister Min?"

Binh shrugged. "Behaving normally, going to work, going home, nothing out of the ordinary, Superintendent. I think he's worried, though. I study him with binoculars and he appears to be uptight."

"Tense and nervous too?"

"Uh, yes, Superintendent."

"Splendid. I trust he's being babysat now."

"He is. Twenty-four-hour shifts have been assigned."

"Binh, you lived in America and were exposed to their slang. Please, do you know what sixish means?"

"Sure," Binh said. "Cocktail hour."

"Beg pardon?"

"Sixish for cocktails, sevenish for dinner."

"Oh. But can sixish be for dinner?"

"If you eat an hour early," Binh said.

An unfamiliar and pleasing aroma of cooked meat, cheese, and spices greeted Kiet at his door. "I hope you like pizza," came a melodic yell from the kitchen.

Pizza? Kiet was weary of playing the hick. "It is one of my favorites," he said, trying to sound urbane and knowing.

Susan came out of the kitchen, holding a spatula. "Good, but where do you find it in Hickorn? there isn't a pizza parlor in town."

"Uh, well," Kiet said, turning his attention to his officers. "Any problems?"

"No, Superintendent," said the one who had delivered Susan's message. "We drove around to many groceries and butcher shops. Nobody followed or caused us any trouble."

"Good night, then. I'll see you in the morning."

The guards left and Susan took Kiet into the kitchen. The dining table was set with plates, wine glasses, and a tablecloth. "Pizza is my soul food. I miss it almost as much at hot bathwater. Dennis once brought me pizza from Bangkok. That was sweet of him, but it was in pretty pathetic shape. Don't mind me. I'm running off at the mouth again."

"You went to the mortuary earlier?"

"He looked like he was sleeping . . ." She caught a tear with her sleeve and opened the oven. "I've forgotten what great therapy cooking is. I'm out of practice. When I'm by myself, I eat out of cans. Dennis always dragged me to expensive restaurants."

She removed a rectangular baking pan that contained a circular, flat, reddish concoction. "Did you know you can't buy a pizza pan in the Kingdom of Luong? I couldn't form the dough perfectly round, but it's close enough."

It was indeed. The red sauce was dotted with chunks of ground meat and mushrooms. White cheese bubbled on top. "It smells wonderful," Kiet said.

"Thanks. I'm crossing my fingers that it tastes as good as it smells. I had to use some Yankee ingenuity. Italian tomato sauce isn't a common item on store shelves and the sausage is a little different. I had to go to four butcher shops to find one who'd grind it per my directions."

The delicious aroma reminded Kiet that he was starving. "You don't have to sell me," he said, glancing at his watch. "Please, let's eat. It's ten minutes past sixish."

They ate, Kiet devouring two-hundred-and-seventy degrees of the circle, Susan the remaining quarter.

"You like?" she asked.

Kiet drained his wine glass and gestured to the empty pan. "I do. I did. There's your evidence."

"Speaking of evidence, what's new on the case?"

Kiet hesitated, unsure how to tell her that police business was confidential, that the disclosure of the rubies was made for effect, and that she should not consider it a sign that he had informally deputized her. But his mood was too mellow from the food and the wine and he was too sympathetic to her loss to be blunt. He evaded the question instead, asking, "You already told me that you never met Mr. McCloud's army colleagues, but did he ever drop the name of an Obon colonel named Marsad Ref?"

"Yeah. That's Mars."

"Excuse me?"

"Dennis called him Mars. That was his nickname to me. I don't think Dennis was afraid of any man, but Mars had him on the verge. I got the impression that Mars was Dennis's bread and butter. Dennis said he was a space case, a mean and rough oddball. Mars, you know, as in the red planet and Martians. Mars was his Second District liaison. When Mars was in Hickorn, I could count on not seeing Dennis."

"Mars," Kiet said, enjoying it.

"That bizarre nickname is all I know, Superintendent Kiet. Dennis kept mum about his flying. Is Mars a suspect?"

Kiet shrugged. "At this point, merely a candidate."

"Dessert?"

"Yes," Kiet said. "Please."

Susan served napoleons, a layered rainbow of jellies, chocolate, and cream. "If Luong had to be colonized, I'm happy it was by people who knew food."

"Me too. At least at this very moment," Kiet mumbled, his mouth full.

"Are you on a personal basis with Prince Pakse?"

"I am."

"I don't suppose you could arrange an interview," she said, smiling at the sight of Kiet inhaling the rich pastry. "An in-depth would clinch my getting the paper past the thesis committee."

"I can try."

"I've struck out. Prince Pakse isn't readily accessible unless you're a general, an ambassador, or a pool shark."

"His Royal Highness is a busy man," Kiet lied.

"You know somebody else I'd like to talk to? And it has nothing to do with my research."

"Who?"

"Sergei Pudkin. I wouldn't pretend to tell you how to solve murders, but his role in this bugs me."

"The rubies," Kiet conceded.

"Yes. If your assumption is right, Dennis died because of them. And I almost did too."

"Provoking a foreign embassy is a serious action. It transcends simple police procedures. If I arrested Pudkin, Russian diplomats and Foreign Ministry personnel would be packed in Headquarters."

"Like sardines."

Kiet nodded. "A tin of sardines that had been opened last week and placed in the sun, demanding this, objecting to that. If they had their way, I'd be walking a beat in Foh Ten."

"Dragon's Bile. I've heard stories, but I don't have the courage to head in there with my tape recorder and notebook. Is it that bad?"

"Worse. Most of the inhabitants are good people. Their crime is poverty. The rest, though—it's a sanctuary for criminals and army deserters."

"The Royal Luongan Military Academy is in the jungle on the other side of Foh Ten," Susan said. "Is that the source of most of the deserters?"

"A sizeable number. They decide the army isn't for them," Kiet said. "They climb a fence. If they flee to

Hickorn or their homes in rural areas, they'll be easily arrested. If they stay in Foh Ten, they've effectively vanished. You have to hate military life to choose that alternative. Colonel Ref was training commandant at the Academy before he went to Obon. Tales of his brutality are legend. He'd survive one hour in Foh Ten. If he was lucky. His former cadets would keep him alive for days if he was not.''

Susan said, "I won't argue with your assumption that the Soviets would protest your arresting a member of their embassy who's in good standing. But Pudkin botched his assignment. He has to be in big, big trouble.''

"I fully expect him to be sent home within a week," Kiet agreed. "A fabricated family emergency or some such.''

"A scientific and engineering attaché fallen from grace," Susan said. "I have an idea.''

"An electronic spy," Kiet said. "A valuable man to lose, but be assured that they will absorb the loss. Your idea, please.''

"Pudkin's electronic background might make it work.''

"Make what work?''

"I took drama courses as an undergrad. I was in several plays. I even played Blanche DuBois. I know how we can spring Pudkin and he'll love us for it.''

"Sydney Greenstreet was the best actor who ever lived," Kiet said. "Your plan, please.''

Susan told him.

"Outrageous," Kiet said.

His cat hopped onto her lap, stretched its jowly head, and licked napoleon goo from her plate. "He's a doll. What's his name?''

"A wretched beast. He deserves no name.''

"Will you?"

Kiet sighed and stood slowly. "Come. If I'm to be exiled to Foh Ten with a nightstick, why not for an insane scheme like this?"

15

SOVIET EMBASSY GUARDS wore short-sleeved khaki devoid of insignia, and caps adorned with a simple silver star mounted in a red band. If they were armed, their weapons were discreetly hidden inside the gate shack. This demeanor of boys-at-camp was Ambassador Kalashnikov's brainstorm, a plank in his campaign to sell Russians in Luong as innocuous guests rather than as hopeful future conquerors.

Bamsan Kiet perceived the guards differently. These fellows were lean and towering and possessed of eyes that saw but did not feel. They spoke clipped, KGB-taught Luongan and if they weren't crack Red Army praetorians, he was Prince Savhana's ghost.

Kiet had shown his identification and said his mission was confidential and of supreme urgency. They regarded his request to see Ambassador Kalashnikov as if Kiet and Susan were Chairman Mao and Chiang Ch'ing, and processed it with polite menace, phoning into the compound several times, receiving several calls in return. Kiet pictured the interior as a prodded hornet's nest.

Eventually they were escorted into the lobby and up a cramped elevator to the ambassador's office.

"Superintendent, an unexpected surprise," Ambassador Kalashnikov said, grinding Kiet's knuckles with a thick paw. "If your urgency involves law and order, I'm puzzled, but I'm at the eager service of my Luongan comrades."

Kiet suppressed a yelp of pain and scanned photographs on the walls. Gorbachev was there, Brezhnev too. Lenin, of course. Stalin this time, Khrushchev not. You couldn't keep track of who in the grave was favored in a given era and who was not. An air conditioner hummed loudly, but accomplished no purpose. What a contradiction, Kiet thought, that America could chill its diplomats into ice cubes, but the world's most frigid nation could not. Except for Kalashnikov's foul Russian cigarette, the ninety-degree, ninety-percent humidity atmosphere was quite agreeable.

Kalashnikov had a cowlick and a bull neck that drooped over his collar. Kiet imagined him as a Ukrainian tractor driver who had been awarded this post on the basis of heroically exceeding threshing quotas. Naturally florid, the ambassador's complexion now had the hue of Susan's pizza sauce. Kiet thought it might be from the effort of pretending that she was invisible.

"My profound apologies for barging in without an appointment, Mr. Ambassador," Kiet said. "It's a hateful task that must be resolved, and I felt it preferable that it should be handled, shall we say, informally."

"Yes, outside of official channels," Kalashnikov replied, still ignoring Susan. "Often that approach is best in delicate situations, which I presume this is. I am an eminently flexible man. Please take seats."

"May I first introduce Mrs. Susan Dempsey-Mohn," Kiet said. "She is the victim of a crime and the object of our intrusion."

"How do you do," Kalashnikov said stiffly, his eyes aimed at the seam between Susan and Kiet.

"Hello," she said meekly. She sniffled loudly then fumbled inside her purse for a tissue.

Not bad for an amateur thespian, Kiet thought, wondering if she was replaying the role of that Blanche DuBois individual. He said, "Mr. Ambassador, I must be blunt. Mrs. Dempsey-Mohn has accused a member of your legation of rape."

"Impossible!" Kalashnikov shouted.

"No disrespect intended, Mr. Ambassador," Kiet said, intending profound disrespect, "but literal interpretation of your denial requires that all male personnel are impotent."

Susan snuffled loudly into her tissue, perhaps concealing a giggle. Kiet cursed himself for snapping at Kalashnikov's irresistible bait. If a cynical remark of his caused her to double up in laughter and spoil their one-act play, he'd be walking a beat in Foh Ten *without* a nightstick.

"I meant that my people are of the highest integrity, the best of a motherland relatively free of crime in its own right. Imperialism is the root of crimes of greed and lust, Superintendent."

"Yes, Mr. Ambassador, but the complainant is adamant. She understands that diplomatic immunity is customarily invoked and that the accused cannot be tried in a Luongan court. Technicalities and treaties, however, do not satisfy her hunger for justice. She is here to verify the event as she has described it to me. She hopes that you will investigate on your own. If you are persuaded that the accused is guilty, she further hopes that he will be punished in a manner appropriate to the penal code of the Union of Soviet Socialist Republics."

Kiet gathered in a lungful of air. Kalashnikov was leaning back in his chair, fingers woven together over an ample midsection, stoically unimpressed with Kiet's monologue. "Who is the accused?"

Kiet performed his part with patience and consulted his notebook. "A scientific and engineering attaché by the name of Sergei Pudkin."

"A good man," Kalashnikov said impassively. "Bright, loyal, hard-working, and a Party member. This charge, I think, is wild and erroneous."

Kiet flipped pages in his notebook, feigning concentration. "Mrs. Dempsey-Mohn reports that Mr. Pudkin had been pestering her for weeks. Although they had never been formally introduced and Mrs. Dempsey-Mohn professes not to have seen him before he began turning up at her door, Mr. Pudkin had evidently become obsessed with her."

"Infatuation is no crime," Kalashnikov said, moving not a muscle.

"Forcible expression of said infatuation is, in Luong, Mr. Ambassador," Kiet said. "Mrs. Dempsey-Mohn alleges that Mr. Pudkin visited her on numerous occasions, pleading for a date. She did not return his overtures. Finally, last night, he burst in, overpowered her, and—"

Susan interrupted him with another loud snuffle.

"On those previous occasions, what was the context of Comrade Pudkin's conversations?" Kalashnikov asked Susan.

"Well, he'd just go on and on 'bout how ah was the fairest thing he ever laid his baby blues on and how ah wasn't givin' him a fair chance to prove he was a gentleman worthy of courtin' me."

Where had Kiet heard that dialect before? It certainly didn't belong to Susan. Was the Yuppie woman speaking in tongues? He remembered: U.S. Ambassador Ritchie, Ambassador Smithson's predecessor. Ritchie was a native of the same subtropical American province as the former president who appointed him.

She continued, "A scant twenty-four hours ago, I reckon he couldn't contain himself any more, cuz he put his shoulder to my door and busted through like the safety chain was linguini, and he, he, he . . ."

Her face dissolved into soggy tissues. Her racking sobs sounded to Kiet too much like "sob." If her performance deteriorated further, he might not live to enjoy suicidal patrols in Foh Ten. But Kalashnikov seemed engrossed. He was wilting, an improbability for a barrel-shaped man apparently composed of pig iron. The pizza sauce had drained from his cheeks and his forearms drooped lazily on armrests.

"The penalty for rape in Hickorn is twenty years in prison," Kiet said. "Diplomatic immunity negates the legalities of determining Sergei Pudkin's guilt or innocence, so, Mr. Ambassador, I leave the matter to your sense of fairness."

"Yes, of course I will conduct my own inquiry," Kalashnikov said blankly. "Who exactly is this allegedly ravaged young lady?"

"Mrs. Dempsey-Mohn is an American college student. She is writing a graduate thesis on Luong. A total innocent. I realize your people have fine credentials, Mr. Ambassador, but her story is quite convincing."

"He threw me down on the floor like ah was a sack of flour, removed my slacks and blouse, and ripped off my undergarments, and . . ." Susan's description was drowned out by her own wailing.

That outburst seemed to arouse Kalashnikov. He sat forward, pizza sauce again flooding his face. "I promise to make inquiries, Miss. Itemization of the alleged assault isn't necessary. Thank you for bringing it to my attention. Now, I request a minute with the superintendent."

Susan whispered a squeaky ver-ah well and left the room. Kalashnikov said to Kiet, "You're being taken in."

"Excuse me?"

"A student? Hah! Kiet, you are a worldly man. Don't you know what her ploy is? She's a spy. A CIA agent in student cover. She isn't studying your history and wildlife. She's documenting your political infrastructure and cataloging your military defenses."

If Luong had military defenses, Kiet hadn't been so informed. "I contemplated that possibility, Mr. Ambassador. We have no dossier on her, however, and the passion of her complaint is compelling."

"You need a national police apparatus, Superintendent. You could have a dossier on *everybody*. I have discussed this with Prince Pakse. I play billiards with him, you know. He beats me every game. He is noncommittal on a national police system. You should speak to him about it. With our help, you could establish an efficient information network. It would be a marvelous tool for you."

"Thank you for the offer, sir, but gossip and rumor are Luongan hobbies. They usually suffice in ordinary crime. Since this case involves foreigners, it is more difficult."

"Look at her, Kiet. Her legs, her breasts, her full lips, her cosmetics and skimpy clothing designed to titillate. Advanced female students in Mother Russia have moustaches and books of mathematical tables," Kalashnikov said hoarsely. "The woman is a slut, a tramp. While she may be no CIA professional, she is the sort readily recruited. She worships the imperialistic gods of money and ambition."

"My mind is open," Kiet said. "I ask only that you satisfy yourself of your Comrade Pudkin's culpability."

Kalashnikov said that he would, and Kiet departed before the man's sexual frustration exploded one of the blood vessels throbbing on his temples. He hurried out of the embassy with Susan.

"A total innocent," she muttered. "Thanks a whole bunch."

"Why were you blathering like a Georgian peanut farmer? Tell me that much, please."

"I couldn't help myself. Blanche DuBois elbowed me

offstage. I once played Eleanor Roosevelt, but she'd hardly do. God, I hope our little skit did the trick! Not even a worm like Pudkin deserves a showdown with King Kong Kalashnikov.''

Kiet opened the passenger door of the Citroën, let Susan in, saw what he hoped to see, and said, "The trick did it. Eyes ahead, please."

Six gear-grinding blocks later, Kiet stopped, flicked on the dome light, reached over the seat, and patted the back of the man curled in a semi-fetal position on the rear seat floor. The man's shirt was torn and bloody from crawling under barbed wire strung above the Soviet Embassy wall. "Sit up. You're safe."

He obeyed and wiped thick glasses on a ripped shirt-sleeve. "You miserable liars. You would do anything to achieve your goals."

"It was her idea," Kiet said.

Susan shrieked in triumph, "I banked on your listening in on Kalashnikov, you being the resident electronics wizard and everything!"

"Comrade Kalashnikov hated me for not bringing you to him," he told Susan. "He was exiling me on next flight."

"Siberia?" Susan said.

"Worse," Pudkin said. "He had me transferred to minor post in North Korea. Pyongyang is guns, concrete, and you can't move without bumping into icon of Kim Il Sung. You depart Comrade Kalashnikov's chambers, I hear his tantrum. He order me took to him. Just the four of us. Him, me, and his two bare hands. He believe you liars, not me, a Young Pioneer and a loyal Party member from the day I enter engineering school. You kill my career. If I not jump window and climb wall, Kalashnikov kill me."

"A regrettable necessity," Kiet said.

"I demand political asylum," Sergei Pudkin said.

Kiet started the car. "Absolutely. That is the final scene of our play."

16

HICKORN POLICE HEADQUARTERS, 900 Avenue Alexandre Loubet, had a secret quirk in its construction that everybody knew. A tunnel built by the Legionnaires connected the French commandant's office to a service door of a storage building on the other side of an adjacent alley. Exit from the office was made through a rotating panel in the bookcase, operated by pulling out a leather-bound volume of Dumas novels.

According to requisition forms now stored in Department archives, the considerable expense was justified by the need for "emergency countermovement and deployment." According to legend, which in Luong was generally far more accurate than any written documentation, the last commandant was a rabbit who worried incessantly about violent revolution and the decline of empire. In the event of rabble pounding on the front gates with machetes, the tunnel afforded escape to the airport and the friendlier climes of Phnom Penh or Hanoi.

The commandant's office belonged to Bamsan Kiet. He had the key to the storage building door. He seldom unlocked the rusty latch and endured the tunnel cobwebs—only when privacy was essential. He led Susan and Pudkin through and shouldered the bookcase with a grunt. He pushed and strained and managed to pivot it free the width of a human body. The French commandant had not designed the mechanism for reverse emergency countermovement and deployment.

Sergei Pudkin's barbed-wire scratches were superficial. Susan daubed them with Mercurochrome. Kiet provided a clean shirt, which hung on the smaller Pudkin like a negligee. With his steel-rimmed glasses and tousled hair, he looked mousy and thoroughly disoriented. He reminded Kiet of Leon Trotsky, Stalin's last rival, who was purged via an axe to the skull in Mexico City in 1940.

Kiet wondered what to do. The idea had been so daring, its execution so perfect. But now he felt like a thief who had stolen a vial of nitroglycerin. Pudkin's application for political asylum was a precedent. If any foreign national had deserted his homeland before in Hickorn, it was news to him. He decided to take advantage of present circumstances and interrogate him, future consequences be damned.

"What was destined for Mrs. Dempsey-Mohn if you had successfully abducted her?"

"Sly gambit," Pudkin said. "You jail me when you sit on me last night, you are in vortex of diplomatic commotion. Advantage is mine. You flee me for my life and advantage is yours. You are chess player, sir? You do police-detecting like Russians play chess. I admire cunning. I am chess master. I take Boris Spassky to thirty-seven moves once in Moscow exhibition tournament."

Kiet looked at Susan. She rolled her eyes. If Sergei Pudkin mistook his bureaucratic caution for cleverness, fine. "Answer my question, please."

"I know not most, but much," Pudkin said. "Russians spy on Russians and rest of world. We spy on Russians with greatest ardor. You discover revisionist attitude and reactionary behavior in man, you own him. I control embassy's listening devices. I can overhear much. I hear Comrade Kalashnikov destructing furniture in rage and spare my own life."

Kiet groaned. "Mr. Pudkin, *please*."

He looked at Susan and bowed. "He see you with binoculars and fall in love or something. Last night not same. He order me to bring you if I have to wrap you in tape and throw you in car trunk."

"Why?"

"You have whereabout of stolen rubies. Your room searched morning after American pilot die. Not there, but you can locate."

"For whom? Ambassador Kalashnikov?" Kiet asked.

"I never pegged him as a closet capitalist," Susan said.

"Not him. He send me on behalf of another. He object, but man say to do. Cannot capture lady's heart with force. Comrade Kalashnikov yell and shout, but finally agree. Extreme move, yes, but he not have choice."

Ril Thoi financing his revolution, Kiet thought. He *knew* Thoi had gone to the Soviet Embassy following the visit to his home. "Kalashnikov's client, please?"

"I am not privy to know, but I do. Man visit in night, in phony disguise. Sum of three or five times I know of. I see man, I tune in Comrade Kalashnikov's office on headphones. My room, where I am under house arrest, I have jacks hidden in wall. Nobody know."

Kiet answered for him, impatiently, "Ril Thoi, Chairman of the Central Committee of the Luongan Communist Party."

Pudkin's eyes seemed to expand to the edges of his magnified lenses. "Thoi! Say Thoi to Comrade Kalashnikov and he have ranting and raving fit over Thoi's independent attitudes. Comrade Kalashnikov never see him in his life. Comrade Kalashnikov send warm greetings of revolutionary solidarity through Thoi's cadres and Thoi ignore. Slap in face. Comrade Kalashnikov give him anything, Thoi merely need ask. Bandages, food, rocket launchers, anything."

Kiet slumped in his chair. "Who, please?"

"Bourgeois colonel of your decadent, feudal kingdom. Ugly man with Swiss bank accounts. You see him and your skin shivers." Pudkin shivered and added, "Murmansk in January."

"Mars, baby," Susan said.

"Lieutenant Colonel Marsad Ref?" Kiet asked.

"Him. Not supposed to know him, but do," Pudkin said, cupping a hand over an ear like a headphone.

"Why would Kalashnikov cooperate with Ref?" Kiet said.

Sergei Pudkin shook his head. "Cannot say in certainty. They careful in Comrade Kalashnikov's office. Ref one time hunt for bugs. Comrade Kalashnikov laugh at him. My heart nearly race out of chest. I nearly run for wall then. He doesn't find. Is no equal to Pudkin for planting bugs. Is bug in frame of beloved Comrade Lenin's picture. I tickle Vladimir Ilyich when I bury it. He smile, he approve."

"Why do you believe the rubies were stolen?"

"Ugly colonel, he say the belong to him and Americans have. He no explain farther. He supposed to do something for Comrade Kalashnikov but he say he no do unless Comrade Kalashnikov help him find rubies. This is extent of my knowing. I cannot listen in all day and all night."

"I'll lock you up and take your case to the Foreign Ministry tomorrow morning," Kiet said.

"In ordinary prisoner cell? No, I beg you! They can pay cutthroats in your jail to kill me."

Susan said, "He might just have a point. Ref has long arms."

"For what you do tonight, you get me dead if you don't protect me. Until I can go to West, you are responsible. You adopt me if you have to."

"The alternative, please?" Kiet said to Susan. "We can't release him."

108

"Do you cook?" Susan asked Pudkin.

The Russian brightened and kissed his fingertips. "Premiere borscht. Bulgar dishes. Stroganoff. I best chef in embassy. Sergei Pudkin is—how you say?—Renaissance man."

Kiet's groan came from the floor of his chest. "An international cooking jamboree in my villa."

Susan unzipped her purse and took out a coin. "We'll flip. Odd person out. Loser gets the couch."

17

BAMSAN KIET AWOKE to the smell of rotting vegetation. His alarm clock indicated eight A.M., an execrable hour considering the length and lateness of yesterday. He dressed, staggered into the bathroom, splashed cold water on his face, and went into the kitchen, the source of the foul odor. Sergei Pudkin was standing at the stove, stirring the contents of an iron pot.

Pudkin grinned and said, "Skimpy larder you have. Must substitute ingredients, but will be gorgeous result."

"Excuse me?"

"Schchi. Meat, cabbages, soured cream. Your milk, it do as the cream. Famous Russian soup."

"For *breakfast?*"

Pudkin lifted out his spoon and offered Kiet a taste. "You try. Marvelous dish. I can cook like nobody. They no permit me in embassy. They have bad cooks so we don't be homesick. Kiet, you defect me to France. Will love Pudkin in Paris."

Kiet backed out of the room. Two uniforms sat nervously on the couch, beside a roll of bedding. Susan had slept there; she called heads and the coin had landed tails. But where were the other two officers he had commandeered at Headquarters on the way home last night? Four good men on shifts, twenty-four hours a day. A minimum requirement for a house transformed into a hostel for material witnesses and defectors.

"The woman is running with our partners," said an officer who read Kiet's anxiety.

"Running," Kiet muttered. He considered tracking her down and ordering her home. Her enemies could eliminate Susan with an automobile "accident" before the guards unholstered their weapons. But no. Denny McCloud's cremation was scheduled at noon. The woman had anxieties of her own to burn off.

"She isn't running anywhere, she's just running," said the befuddled cop. "I don't understand, but Lo and Phi have forty-fives and M-16s. They will protect her with their lives."

Kiet pictured Lo and Phi struggling to keep up with the sleek Yuppie, gasping and perspiring, their rifles carried at port arms, heavy by now as lead. He instructed the officers to compliment Pudkin's cooking and try to ignore the strange aromas. "If he's happily domestic," Kiet whispered, "we don't have to worry about him wandering."

Kiet drove to Headquarters for refuge, but saw from outside the gate that none would be forthcoming. Parked at the door was a Mercedes sedan he recognized. It belonged to a high-level official of the Foreign Ministry. Obviously, Ambassador Kalashnikov figured out the ruse and had already applied pressure to gain return of his scientific and engineering attaché.

Attacks of indecision and heartburn struck simultaneously. Kiet put the Citroën in neutral and chewed an antacid tablet. The medicine soothed his sour stomach, but had no effect on its cause. Kalashnikov's quick reaction was unexpected. Kiet had no delaying tactics prepared and it was much too early in the day to deal with an overwrought bureaucrat.

Captain Binh quickstepped out of the building and into his car, saving him. "Superintendent, Deputy Foreign Minister in Charge of Eastern Affairs Mun Tai is—"

Kiet held up a hand. "Inquiring as to the status of a Sergei Pudkin."

Binh nodded excitedly. "Yes, A defecting Russian. What is going on, Superintendent? Tai has been screaming at me and I don't know—"

Kiet raised his other hand, then told the story.

"At *your* villa, Superintendent?"

"In some cultures, if you rescue a man from death, you are required to adopt him," Kiet said. "I know this from *National Geographic*. I created an inverse responsibility. If Pudkin dies, I killed him."

Binh whistled through tense lips. "Colonel Ref and the Russians. He should be shot for treason."

"I would gladly roll up my sleeves and fill the sandbags, but treason is not easily proven."

"Another development, Superintendent. Minister of Defense Cuong Van sent a messenger, asking that you see him at your earliest convenience. I saw you and slipped away, thinking that you would prefer to attend to Minister Van's request immediately."

"Superior judgment on your part, Captain. Absolutely splendid. I don't compliment your decision-making abilities often enough. Come with me, please."

Binh blushed and smiled. "Thank you. Minister Van is a hero of mine."

"One problem, though. In your absence, who will babysit Deputy Minister Tai?"

"Sergeant Fri, Superintendent. Tai yells at him and Fri yells louder."

Kiet smiled contentedly and ground the shift lever into gear.

Bamsan Kiet and Cuong Van were old friends and *lycée* classmates. Prior to his appointment as minister of defense, Van served as commander in chief of the Royal Luongan Army. Kiet had been delighted by the promotion. Van, a first cousin of His Royal Highness, was loyal, competent, and scrupulously honest. He had extinguished numerous coup d'etat attempts before they could catch fire, several with Kiet's aid.

His upper-floor office in the Ministry overlooked Mu Savhana, otherwise known as the Street of Flowers for the rainbow of perennial blooms in its wide median, a photogenic sight that had become a staple in travel brochures. Mu Savhana ended to the south a short block from the main entrance to the Royal Palace. The Ministry's immediate northern neighbor was the National Bank.

The building was France's last Hickorn edifice, a rather ordinary three-story cube decorated with upswept overhangs in the pagoda style. The French had planned it as a trade pavilion, but Independence interrupted its completion. An infant military bureaucracy with a need for space rapidly moved in. To this day cornices were missing and window sashes were naked of trimwork. Kiet regarded the Ministry as monstrously ugly, a belated architectural compromise by colonists who finally realized that they were governing Hickorn, not Marseilles.

"Bosha, you've been a whirling dervish lately," said Minister of Defense Cuong Van. "Everybody I talk to, it's Kiet this, Kiet that."

Kiet stared innocently.

"The murdered American, his girlfriend, and now this Russian you liberated. Law enforcement is indeed an exciting profession."

Cuong Van's appearance was deceptive. Short and slender, he wore glasses as thick as his hair was thin. Yet his body hadn't deviated a kilogram in weight or a degree in muscle tone since he starred as a center-forward on the Luongan national soccer team. Kiet credited some of Van's success to underestimation. Political and military opponents of the 1980s were caught as figuratively flat-footed as when Van streaked around Pakistani and Cambodian fullbacks in the 1950s.

"Ah, rumors and gossip."

"Are they true, Bosha?"

"Percentages would dictate that they are." Kiet cleared his throat and added, "Hickorn gossip is uncannily accurate."

"Binh, is it not?" Cuong Van said. "Aren't you the young man who studied police techniques in the United States? We anticipate great things from you."

Captain Binh was too gaga in the presence of Luong's top soldier to reply.

"Bosha, I'm worried about my Second Military District command."

"How so?"

"General Vo is incommunicative. Not that we were ever Siamese twins, but this week he has been cold and evasive. I've received reports outside the chain of command from officers unwaveringly loyal to me. They say Obon is in turmoil. Vo is as nervous as a civet cat. He assigns constant patrols that have no cogent mission. My eyes and ears in the field generate fragments, incomplete reports, but without exception the bits and pieces correlate to your murdered Mr. McCloud. They must. There have been no other factors disturbing the status quo."

Kiet took the rubies from his pocket. The envelope was almost worn out. He sprinkled them on Cuong Van's desk and told everything he knew. Van seemed to age as he digested the news. He said, "I've tolerated General Vo's Obon fiefdom as a lesser evil, Bosha. He is a buffer between us and the Rouge and the opium industry. If I acted on my personal dislike for him and what he does, I would have retired him years ago, but Prince Pakse and I are in agreement that a confrontation could precipitate

114

a civil war. Superpowers would leap in and choose sides. I have nightmares of Hickorn emulating Saigon."

"No argument there, Cuong."

"That lunatic, Ref! If we hadn't manipulated him out of the Academy, he would have killed cadets. I guess I shouldn't be surprised that he has an arrangement with the Russians. Ref and those rubies, yes, but what's in it for Kalashnikov? And where does our old school chum, Ril Thoi, fit into the equation?"

"I don't know," Kiet said. "My investigation advances in stages that provide more tangles and more questions than answers."

"Bosha, I need your experience and cunning. I'm a soldier, not a *gendarme* or a spy. I can snap my fingers and send a division of troops into battle. But against whom? A few greedy men are undermining the Kingdom. How do we counterattack?"

"Divide and conquer," Captain Binh said.

The older men looked at him. Please, Kiet thought, no inspirations involving computers or polygraphs or Miranda warning cards.

"Go on," Van said.

"Well, sir, uh, gentlemen," Binh said nervously, "your Siamese twin remark, Mr. Minister, gave me an idea. If anybody concerned is a set of Siamese twins, it's General Vo and Colonel Ref. Perhaps they can be separated. I'm thinking of the Rouge ambush."

"A highly dubious feat of heroism," Cuong Van said, nodding at Kiet.

"I know, but Luong is abuzz over it. It's knocked everybody's socks off," Binh said.

The forcible removal of one-and-a-half-million pairs of stockings, Kiet wondered? Binh would be ideal as a translator of Susan Dempsey-Mohn's idiom, him and his year in America.

"Whatever's happening is coming down soon," Binh

continued, talking fast. "If Ref's brought to Hickorn, taking the character of both men in consideration, suspicion will occur. They can't possibly trust each other. One will worry that the other is deviating from the master plan, whatever it may be, for his own end and cutting the other out of the deal."

"I like your idea," Kiet said, proud of his young adjutant. "How do we accomplish this?"

"The Order of Savhana. Invite Ref to Hickorn and present it to him in an elaborate ceremony. His ego would not permit him to refuse."

Luong's highest award for bravery," Cuong Van said, massaging his forehead with both hands. "Wherever Prince Savhana's grave is, the earth shall tremble."

"I like it," Kiet said. "His ghost will sympathize with our dilemma and forgive us."

A major in fatigue uniform knocked and entered. His heels clicked together and he handed the minister of defense a note. "Captain, one of your people is outside with an important message. Go. I compliment you for your creativity."

Binh excused himself and left with a giddy expression. Kiet was certain that his feet weren't touching the ground.

"A brilliant but temporary solution," Van said. "Your Captain Binh has enormous potential."

"He does. With the proper retraining," Kiet said. "And his idea suggests a longer-lasting solution."

"Does it require that we spit on our heritage again? The Order of Savhana has been conferred only four times during my thirty years of service, Bosha. All four awards were posthumous. Those men didn't sacrifice themselves against the Rouge for smuggled rubies."

"I'm afraid it requires that we spit on your table of organization. While Marsad Ref is in town for his medal, further reward his bravery by promoting him to full colonel and reassign him to a harmless desk job."

Cuong Van thought it over and laughed. "I'll institute a new postion. Deputy Chief of Staff in Charge of Strategic Support Materiel."

"Which means?"

"Marsad Ref will have supreme authority in the realm of purchasing toilet paper and jeep tires and the ilk for the entire Royal Luongan Army."

"How will he accept this alleged promotion?"

Cuong Van tapped the collar of his white shirt. "A third silver pip goes with the job. He can't decline. A month or two from now, yes, he'll be dissatisfied, but maybe our problem will be resolved by then."

"What you've told me about Brigadier General Vo is encouraging, Cuong. He's suffering from galloping paranoia. He's apt to make a mistake and Ref will be here under your thumb."

"Good. Let's hope so. Bosha, the street redesignation ceremony takes place in less than a week. Avenue Mao Tse-tung to Avenue Ronald Reagan has the potential to offend. Is security going to be a problem?"

"It shouldn't be. Every man in my department will be on duty."

"If that's not sufficient, I can lend you troops. A company, a battalion. Just ask."

"Appreciated."

Binh burst into the room. His feet were solidly on the carpet. Gravity had also slumped the euphoria from his face. To Kiet he looked as if his mother had just died.

"Superintendent, Lon Min is gone."

Kiet groaned. "Almost as bad."

"Pardon me, Superintendent?"

"Never mind. What do you mean by gone?"

"He was driving along Ma San Boulevard half an hour ago. We had a surveillance car behind him. It was in communication with a second unit by radio. All of a sudden, Min increased speed. He stopped sideways at the Foh Ten Bridge, blocking both lanes. He jumped out, ran across the bridge, and disappeared into Foh Ten.''

"Your men didn't pursue?'' Kiet asked.

"The officer in the lead car was by himself, Superintendent,'' Binh said defensively. "What would you do?''

"No criticism intended,'' Kiet said. He turned to Van. "Does your offer of soldiers apply to this?''

Van pushed his intercom buzzer. "Two platoons, Bosha, outfitted with automatic weapons. They're yours until Lon Min is found. I wouldn't stick a toe into Foh Ten with anything less.''

18

TWENTY-FOUR HOURS LATER, Lon Min's murdered body
was found in a Foh Ten bar. Bamsan Kiet was on the
roof of the Hickorn Continental when the message was
delivered to him and he accepted the news with resignation. To the famished wolves of Foh Ten, Lon Min was a
rabbit, whatever valuables he carried torn from him like
tender flesh.

"I don't get it," Susan said. "I assume he knew he
was being followed, but there must have been a million
less hazardous ways of ditching his tail."

"Agreed," Kiet said. They were standing on the flat
roof center, at a low railing that divided it from the
sloping red tiles. Kiet had been considering using the
position as a command post for the ceremony. Rue Ho
Chi Minh and Avenue Mao Tse-tung met a block north
and this was the highest vantage point in the immediate
area. Three men with binoculars and radios could do the
job of ten patrolling at street level.

He had invited Susan along. He figured that if she did
her research with him, he need not worry about restlessness overcoming good judgment, she and her notepad
and her camera doing something rash. Cuong Van, mean-
while, had built a wall of influence between Sergei Pudkin and the Foreign Ministry. For the time being, angry
demands would be deflected with courtesy and ineffi-
ciency. The Soviet defector, at the moment, was merrily

cooking blintzes at Kiet's villa, undisturbed by diplomats bearing summonses.

"Are you going to Foh Ten?"

"Yes, Captain Binh is waiting for me at the bridge."

She locked an arm around one of his. "Take me, please. This might be my only chance to see Dragon's Bile. If you say no, you'll have to pry me off you with a crowbar."

Kiet felt her soft shape, smelled her perfume. While he knew nothing sexual was intended by the contact, his body was firing confused signals to his brain. His wife, Tien, had been a clinger, a hugger. Twenty years had passed and he could still feel the imprint of her snuggling. Not that he had remained celibate after her death, but frenzied, anonymous couplings had lost their appeal years ago and mature women with designs couldn't dislodge a bachelor's routine.

He gently pushed her to arm's length and said, "Very well. With conditions. The Nikon stays. Your purse too." He touched a dangling earring—a clunky silver and mother-of-pearl affair that resembled a fishing lure. "Especially those."

"There's an awful reason why you're telling me this," she said.

"Luong's climate," Kiet said. "It's never cool enough to keep car windows rolled up. People will reach in and grab anything they can sell for a kilo of rice. If an earlobe is taken with a bauble, it can be removed before presenting the treasure to a buyer."

"But you're the *police,*" Susan said, wide-eyed. "Wouldn't they be afraid to?"

"Fear is inversely proportional to the time span since your last meal," Kiet said. "Your purse or camera is snatched and the thief vanishes into a slum more densely populated than Calcutta. And Foh Ten nine-year-olds are quicker than cats."

"If you can't catch them on the spot, how about locating them through witnesses?"

Kiet opened the roof door for her. "Never in the history of Foh Ten has there been a witness. Come."

Your nose told you that you were in Foh Ten. There was no sewage system and garbage was constantly picked through, too precious to be trucked off. Streets were not even alleys, they were wide paths between shanties. Most dwellings were constructed of cardboard and tin. As a consequence, exterior walls were printed with a repetition of Coca-Cola, Honda, and Toshiba logos. Mapping Foh Ten was an impossibility. Its thoroughfares shifted like the tributaries of the Ma San River during monsoon season.

Binh drove the Citroën. Kiet and Susan rode with him. They followed on the bumper of a Capital Military District jeep manned by troops with automatic rifle barrels spiked menacingly in the air. The trip was slow, almost a walking pace. Inhabitants cared none for the concept of traffic.

"What's that pear-shaped thingie on the tip of his gun?" Susan asked, pointing at a soldier in the jeep.

"A grenade launcher," Kiet said.

"He wouldn't actually use it, would he?"

"I hope not," Kiet said. "It's mainly for show."

"My ex-husband was a lawyer. His firm handled a lot of criminal defense cases. He said cops he knew preferred to go into a tense situation or a bad neighborhood kind of low-key. It was part macho, but they didn't want to show too much force either."

"Macho? We're merely saying that we do not want to die. If they respect that desire, we'll respect them."

"They walk in front of us and don't even look," Susan said.

"They know we won't hit them," Kiet said. "If we

do, the paperwork is immense. They know us better than we know them."

"That's cynical," Susan said sharply. "Who is *they* and why isn't anybody caring for them? Luong has no social services program I know of, but it should."

"Excuse me?"

"Welfare," Binh piped up. "In America, if you can't work or if you claim you can't work, you receive a monthly check in the mail. It's amazing. They have these people known as Welfare Queens. Before they're caught, they collect hundreds of thousands of dollars by having checks sent to post office boxes under a multitude of pseudonyms."

"In Luong, welfare is family," Kiet said. "When you're unable to provide for yourself, your children and brothers and uncles take you into their homes. Either these people have no kin or they've alienated them. Some are sick, some are feeble, some are lazy and criminal, many have committed the crime of growing old. You have no slums in Chicago or New York or Seattle?"

"We do. Sure. But at least there's effort at every government level to improve the living conditions of the poor and elderly. Social Security, for instance."

"I sympathize with the impoverished, but our government is too poor to supply a dole. The Americans and Russians generously offer us bullets and lengthened runways."

Susan exhaled heavily. "I've been here long enough to realize that everything you've said is true, but sometimes it just doesn't sink in even when I see it."

"Kipling's assertion," Kiet said.

The sociological tilt of the conversation was giving him a headache. He asked Binh, "Did you notify Plaset Curj of Lon Min's demise?"

"I did, Superintendent, minutes prior to meeting you. I offered to release him from jail."

"Ah," Kiet said. "With his superior among the departed, there is no case."

"He pleaded to stay. He said he'd be killed too."

"And you said?"

"I told him he could remain our guest if he would reciprocate the favor."

Kiet smiled. "I imagine he's still talking."

"I had to admonish him to slow down, Superintendent. He was talking so fast and in such a shrill tone, the stenographer couldn't keep up."

"Did he divulge anything particularly interesting?"

"I had to go. I'll study the transcript later," Binh said. "There was one thing that stuck in my mind, though, Plaset Curj saw Lon Min and Marsad Ref together shortly before Denny McCloud's scheduled eight o'clock takeoff. That's the essence of it. Curj was confessing impure thoughts in grammar school. his sordid life's story from birth. I doubt if there's much else we'll benefit from. Here we are."

"Mars is coming around like a boomerang again," Susan said. "The man who is everywhere."

They stopped at one of Foh Ten's more substantial structures. Odd-sized corner timbers supported a thatched roof, bamboo walls, and wooden window shutters. There was no sign on the building and no front door. Men of various ages were inside, seated at tables, playing cards, drinking glasses of iced beer. Soldiers stood at the bar, hands tight on the shoulder straps of their slung rifles. Troops and bar customers maintained a truce by avoiding prolonged eye contact. The sprinkling of women at the tables, Kiet observed, were young, but plain and listless, several cuts inferior to the sensual Continental *terrasse* whores. A hard-bitten, older woman with heavy breasts tended bar.

"Ice in beer is a new one on me," Susan said.

Kiet told her, "Foh Ten has no electricity, therefore

no refrigeration. Ice carts with armed guards bring it in from the city and sell it chunk by chunk."

"This place can't be locked," Susan said before they entered. "They must steal it blind."

"No," Binh said. "It belongs to one of the gang bosses who control Foh Ten. No random crime here."

"Where is Lon Min?" Kiet asked, walking in.

Binh gestured to a curtained doorway behind the bar. "There are stalls and bunks the girls and their johns use. Lon Min was in one. The soldiers who searched said he looked as if he was sleeping. That is, until they noticed a small-caliber bullet hole in the back of his head. In America, the newspapers would term it an execution-style slaying."

"There must be fifty people in this dive," Susan said to Binh. "Superintendent Kiet informs me that witnesses don't exist in Dragon's Bile."

"Unfortunately true," Binh said with a humorless smirk. "Nobody saw Lon Min come in. Nobody had ever seen him before, either. Nobody heard a gunshot. If this was Washington, D.C., we could force the proprietor to cooperate. We could put him out of business."

"And you can't here?"

Kiet shrugged and answered, "The gang boss would merely move. He wouldn't care. A minor inconvenience. There is no property ownership in Foh Ten. You occupy space. If you're strong, you hold on to it. If you're forced to relocate, you take the space occupied by someone weaker."

"Shouldn't you question the woman behind the bar, anyway?" Susan asked Kiet. "She seems to be the manager."

"If you wish," he said wearily. And so he did.

Skintight Levi jeans did not flatter skinny legs and a wide torso. Breasts inside a V-necked blouse sagged like thick sausages. In this kingdom of lithe, flat-chested women, highly salable assets in her younger days, Kiet thought.

"No, sorry," she said, "It's busy and noisy, day and night."

"Of course," Kiet said.

"Shall we view the body, Superintendent?" Binh asked.

"Well," Kiet said, rummaging for an excuse. "Are you recommending an autopsy by Dr. Pho?"

"It couldn't hurt, although on examination I didn't see evidence of torture or a scuffle," Binh said.

"Then inspection of Min by another layman would be repetitious," Kiet said.

Susan nudged him. "If I didn't know better, I'd think you were squeamish."

Captain Binh laughed at the joke. Kiet managed a chuckle and said that they could discuss plans outside.

The bartender had been eying Kiet, the only man in his contingent wearing civilian clothes. "Is she your concubine?" she asked, looking at Susan.

"No."

"Royal troops are cheapskates," she said. "Foh Ten scum is cheaper. You look like you got money. See me tonight. You'll like. She's too young for you. This concubine of yours, she's as flat as a boy."

Kiet disagreed. Like all other things, mammary volume was relative. He dared not speak.

Susan had no such reticence. "Hey, wait a—"

Kiet took Susan's arm. "Come."

The woman lifted her blouse up. "This or a boy? If you like her better, you like boys."

"Bitch," Susan yelled.

Bar patrons were watching in amusement, diverted from dull card games, diluted beer, and whores few of them could afford. Kiet pulled Susan outside.

Red in the Yuppie's face blotted out her tan. "She's so ugly she could stop a cuckoo clock."

"Yes, yes, please," Kiet said. "Please remember that this is Foh Ten, not *Lé Avenue*. Binh, what are your conclusions about the death of the associate deputy minister of transportation?"

"I am puzzled. His pockets were empty."

"Robbery?"

"That was my initial assumption, but he was wearing a gray business suit, white shirt, and blue tie. And there are traces of an adhesive substance on his cheeks, jaw, and upper lip."

Kiet began to understand. "What was he wearing when you lost him yesterday?"

"Tan slacks and an expensive pullover. Italian, if I'm not mistaken."

"So his body is dressed appropriately for a funeral or an international flight. And the adhesive is possibly from a false beard."

Binh said, "That's my guess."

"He might pass through Hickorn International Airport unrecognized in such a disguise," Kiet said. "False identity papers and a pocket full of money would complete the deal."

"Lon Min wasn't stupid or crazy, Superintendent. He was too smart to run into Foh Ten unless he thought—"

"He had a sanctuary and a guaranteed and profitable escape from Luong," Kiet finished.

"He was double-crossed and shot?" Susan said.

"He knew too much," Binh said in a somber voice that reminded Kiet of a Sydney Greenstreet role. But what was the name of that movie?

"I was wrong about Foh Ten witnesses," Kiet said to Susan. "Dragon's Bile opens its arms to dead ones."

19

THE KINGDOM OF LUONG was not yet enlightened by the miracle of television. Since Bamsan Kiet had never traveled beyond its borders, his knowledge of the small screen was confined to bubbling descriptions by Binh, who missed this aspect of America even more than instant cheeseburgers.

The young adjutant's enthusiasm seemed peculiar to Kiet. Prime-time "soap operas" whose story lines focused on fraud and adultery. Sporting events in which videotape replays coaxed criticism of referee decisions. Violent dramas where automobiles were customarily destroyed in chases. Celebrity status conferred on men and women who smiled at cameras and read news copy.

Why did Binh yearn for the "tube," as he called it, when Hickorn's twenty-some motion-picture theaters regularly featured Sydney Greenstreet, Sabu, and Doris Day? And why had American television sapped his enjoyment of radio, a wonderfully simple medium that demanded only your ears and your imagination?

Two of Luong's three radio stations transmitted from Hickorn, the third from Obon. The Obon station's antenna tower was blown up by the Rouge in 1982, their most successful action of the eighties. Repairs were patchwork, the owner's attitude being that an investment blasted into rubble again was a fool's purse. It had operated intermittently since.

Kiet's favorite Hickorn station was privately owned.

Occidental hit tunes by the Beatles and Slim Whitman played twelve hours a day. As Kiet drove Susan to his villa and returned to Headquarters with Binh, he listened to the other, a station subsidized by the Ministry of Information. Kiet objected not to its music—traditional Luongan melodies and operas—but to the commentary. The reporting was usually dull and long-winded, bordering on propaganda.

They were broadcasting from Hickorn International Airport. Lieutenant Colonel Marsad Ref had arrived from Obon and was being honored for his dazzling victory against the Luong Rouge. Minister of Defense Cuong Van presided. According to the somber announcer, the ceremony was nearing its conclusion. Ref had been awarded the Order of Savhana and Minister Van was pinning on the honored's collar the insignia of a full colonel.

Kiet felt bad for his old friend, aware how distasteful this charade was for him. The Hickorn Symphony could be heard in the background. Maybe empathy was affecting his ears, but the drums sounded hollow, the trumpets like castrated geese. He switched off the radio.

"In the United States, reporters have portable cameras," Binh said. "We could be watching this live."

Kiet shot him a hard and sour glance.

"That is, if a person had nothing better to do than sit in front of a television," Binh said prudently.

Kiet and Binh read Plaset Curj's confession, fifteen typewritten pages of penitence. Binh was right: In his despair, Curj had unloaded a lifetime's worth of guilt, the majority of the sins so petty they were comical. It was as if Binh had been the doorkeeper at a Christian Heaven.

They sifted the adrenaline-soaked gibberish. The remarks about seeing Lon Min and Marsad Ref together

128

just prior to McCloud's scheduled takeoff settled out. "Potentially helpful," Kiet said. "It confirms what I'd presumed, but Lon Min told Curj to mind his own business and he obeyed."

"Min and Ref strolled out of Curj's view," Binh said. "They were headed in the direction of McCloud's Caribou."

"End of story," Kiet said. "Curj didn't see the murder. He wouldn't be alive if he had. He signed papers verifying a thousand kilos of rice and kept his eyes on his desktop. What is that Biblical tale about those depraved cities? Run from them as fast as you can, but don't look back or you'll become a pillar of salt. Plaset Curj completed his shift and went home, thankful he was still flesh and blood."

"Do you believe Lon Min was with Ref on McCloud's plane, Superintendent?"

"And risk blood spattering on his Guccis? No. His duty was to insure Ref's privacy, to insure that no airport personnel would stumble upon the killing. He performed his job well."

"How do we nab him?" Binh said, slamming a fist into a palm. "We know he's guilty, but we haven't an ounce of concrete evidence."

"Is it not the same in America?" Kiet asked. "*Time* magazine frequently writes about the Mafia. Prosecution of those thugs is impossible unless disgruntled organization members step forward, and if you volunteer testimony, you will likely have a fatal accident on the eve of the trial. Ref and the opium and the shiny things in my pocket, isn't he and his business our Mafia? He and Lon Min and Dennis McCloud, too?"

"They've been prosecuting and imprisoning mafiosi in the past few years, Superintendent."

"Splendid. How?"

"You just said how," Binh replied glumly.

"Ah," Kiet said. "Luong crime busting is no different. We require luck and we require reliable informants. This case has a scarcity of each."

A clerk came in with a note for Kiet. He said it had been brought by an army lieutenant who stiffly declined to wait for a answer. Kiet looked at it and said to Binh, "I've been invited by Colonel Ref to have cocktails with him at the Continental. At my soonest convenience."

"Ref doesn't invite," Binh said. "He summons."

"Ref will never be our reliable informant," Kiet said, "but he may be our luck."

Binh was concerned. "Superintendent, the man's dangerous. I'd better trail along with—"

"No," Kiet said. "Thank you, but I'll be fine. Luck is too easily spoiled."

Tables on the *terrasse* had been joined for Ref and his large and loud entourage, eight or ten of them cutting an arrogant swath through the middle. They had the lounge area to themselves, other customers driven off by the inevitability of rowdyism. Jittery waiters scampered to and from the bar and kitchen, refilling glasses and plates. The scene struck Kiet as medieval—a king and his court.

Kiet took a corner table and waited. His pride would not allow him to approach Ref, as if a subject reporting for his audience. The colonel's party was composed of army officers equal to or junior in rank to him, with a seasoning of LaCroix's most beauteous whores. The inferior status of the guests didn't surprise him. Ref had already received formal praise from generals and ministers at the airport and he was the type who absorbed energy from toadies.

A pitcher of Golden Tiger draft beer was brought to Kiet, compliments of Colonel Ref. Kiet gave the waiter five thousand-zin notes and asked him to thank the colonel anyway. Drinking on his own money at outrageous prices would be a disincentive to drink himself silly. If Ref's strategy was to ignore him until he was in a stupor, the colonel would instead have his audience with a police superintendent who was only bored and drowsy.

He had finished a third of the pitcher and all but a morsel of the fried shrimp he'd ordered when Marsad Ref came over and sat down.

"If I weren't in such a happy mood, I'd be insulted that you refused my gift," Ref said.

He wore dress whites, triple silver pips of a full colonel gleaming on shoulder boards. The nickel-plated Colt automatics Kiet had seen at Obon hung from a patent-leather pistol belt. Mirrored sunglasses, of course.

"No insult intended, colonel, but members of my department, regardless of rank, aren't allowed to accept gratuities, no matter how small or innocent."

"Who made that stupid rule?"

"Me," Kiet said.

"Appearances are important," Ref conceded, missing the point entirely. "What I wanted to speak to you about, Kiet, is your murder investigation."

"Excuse me. Which murder?" Kiet said, squinting in false sincerity. He wanted to laugh, hoping he wouldn't. The Golden Tiger was getting to him after all. Maybe the Westerners' Amber Death nickname *was* valid.

"When you visited us, Kiet, you promised General Vo that you would inform him of progress on the McCloud case. I'm asking you as a favor to him. You said that McCloud's mail slot here was stuffed with telegrams from a Bangkok gem dealer and that the gem dealer claimed ignorance. Is there any progress on that front?"

Kiet remembered his lie. He evaded. "General Vo so generously promised to be on the alert for black-market jewels. Is there any progress on *that* front?"

Ref looked at him, lips pursed as tightly as jaws on a

vise. The man's face was leathery, a glove-soft beardless leather, the skin stretched over sunken cheekbones like drum membranes. Kiet felt goose bumps.

"No, Kiet. No progress. We checked with the soldiers on McCloud's last flight. They have no information. They saw nothing incriminating."

"May I have their names, Colonel? I prefer to interview them myself. Congratulations, by the way, on your promotion and decoration for heroism."

"Thank you. The names, no. Troop movements are classified. Army business. You should know that. The Bangkok gem dealer, you should be interviewing him."

"Alas, we tried," Kiet said, creating as he went. "The Bangkok police were notified. They reported that the gem dealer had fled the country. They knew of him, though. He had long been suspected of ruby smuggling."

"Rubies," Ref said evenly.

Kiet crossed his legs, feeling the sharp facets of the stones in his pocket. "Perplexing. As General Vo stated, Luong hasn't a crystal of cloudy quartz in its soil."

"On a different note, you're rumored to be hiding a Russian defector. Is he connected to the killing?"

"The McCloud killing or the Lon Min killing? If you haven't heard, Min was murdered in Foh Ten sometime yesterday."

"Lon Min," Ref said. "The name is familiar."

"I should think it is," Kiet said. "Associate Deputy Minister of Transportation Min was also manager of Hickorn International Airport."

"That's right. I knew the name from somewhere."

Kiet noticed that the pitcher was half full and that the glass in his hand was empty. Ref's ability to fluster was notorious, but Kiet was neither frightened nor even wary. Thanks to the Golden Tiger and Ref's denials, his predominant emotion was anger. He said, "Two of your dearest friends died violently within a week, Colonel

132

Ref. You exhibit no outward signs of grief. I admire your strength, sir, and your self-control. Myself, I would be a weepy wreck.''

"I made a mistake sending you a big pitcher of beer, Kiet. You can't hold your alcohol. You're speaking in hallucinations. Next, you'll be pissing your pants.''

Kiet laughed. "Dennis McCloud is also a complete stranger?''

"He worked for us. He was no friend. He betrayed our trust by smuggling opium.''

"Opium isn't the only commodity he smuggled, Colonel.''

"What commodity are you referring to, Kiet? These phantom jewels of yours?''

"That information is classified, sir. Police business. You should know that. I'll advance a theory, though. McCloud's killer was such a vicious butcher and was so engrossed in his sadism that his search was incomplete.''

"Are you telling drunken riddles or are you making accusations?''

Ref's face was a stone mask. It reminded Kiet of an evil icon in Luongan mythology, an unliving creature responsible for crop-ruining floods or droughts, depending on its whim. Smash the stone form and vipers would crawl out. If the hero of the myth didn't kill the vipers before they killed him, the populace suffered another season of starvation. "Forgive me, Colonel. I'm so intoxicated I'm seeing snakes.''

"You're talking like a crazy man, Kiet, but I know you aren't. I think you're teasing me. What else do you think you know?''

"I know that the McCloud case is steering me to a series of dead ends. The Lon Min case is fresh. It's conjecture and likely to remain so. My adjutant and I compare these killings to Mafia murders.''

"What is Mafia?''

"A powerful and impenetrable organization of European and American criminals."

"You're the police expert. Are you claiming Luong has one of these Mafias?"

"Oh, perhaps that and beyond, but if a Mafia exists in the Kingdom, politics are combined."

"Politics?"

"Communist politics, Colonel. Possibly."

"The Rouge?"

"Our enemies who tremble before Colonel Marsad Ref? Probably not. The Soviet variety, Ambassador Kalashnikov as a principal."

"Your Russian defector?"

"Classified information, sir. Sorry."

Ref clamped a hand on Kiet's forearm. From a distance, it might appear as a friendly gesture of male camaraderie. It was not.

"Listen good, Kiet. I'm tolerating you because General Vo asked me to follow up on your McCloud investigation. I invited you in sincerity and you insult and mock me."

Ref was trying to touch thumb to fingertips. Only bone obstructed, and the Golden Tiger in Kiet's system was an inadequate anesthetic. Kiet resolved not to lose face. He fixed his eyes on Ref's chromium lenses and said, "I love Hickorn and my position. If a person kills a person in my city, that person will be punished by our laws."

"Kiet, you're acting stupid and you're as smart as you're sane. You say the McCloud murder is a series of dead ends. All right. Close your file and police what you're capable of policing. Capture a couple of those urchins who snatch Rolexes from the wrists of foreigners and shoot them. I'm assigned to Hickorn and I won't be a colonel buried in a staff job for long. The police and the army should be allies. Do you understand what I'm telling you?"

Pain radiated through Kiet's arm, but Ref had just numbed it slightly. He was offering a reconciliation, his version of a bribe. Power instead of money. Life over death.

Hooting and hollering from Ref's party spared him. The toadies and whores were demanding good-naturedly that their hero return. Fun was impossible without him. Ref released Kiet's arm. Kiet dragged it across the table, like a small game animal inflicted with a spinal injury. He wanted to flex his hand, to see if he could, but he didn't.

"What do you say, Kiet?" Ref said, rising.

The colonel had presented a deal, a vague offer. He wouldn't have if Kiet's probing hadn't worried him. Herewith—luck.

"Have a nice day," Kiet said.

20

KIET'S RESOLUTION TO cease drinking in the daytime was once again belated. Binh had brought home from the District of Columbia an Americanism that applied, something to do with horses departing a corral, but Kiet's mind was too woozy to mesh the analogy. His head throbbed, though compared to the fire in his arm, it was a mere twinge.

Luckily, Marsad Ref had demonstrated his manhood on Kiet's left arm. He was able to steer and shift gears through Hickorn's manic traffic with his right. It was not a smooth ride, nor was it kind to the Citroën's transmission, but he didn't care.

Reaching his villa was a singular goal. He badly needed a siesta. This would be his first in years. There was a suggestion of tropical torpor in the custom that he found offensive. He prided himself on working the nine-to-five schedule of developed countries, and whatever else was required. Today was an exception. Everybody deserved an exception, he told himself.

He walked inside and knew that peace and slumber were not to be his. A guard approached and said in a quavering voice, "Superintendent, I know your instructions about turning away anyone—"

"Who's here?"

The officer thrust a document at him. "Deputy Minister of Defense Doa. This is signed permission by Minister

Van. I assumed it would be proper. I examined him for weapons and he had none."

Kiet read the note. It looked like Cuong Van's handwriting, but he had never heard of anybody important at Defense called Doa. He thought of another Binh Americanism involving glass houses and vandalism, and resisted haranguing the officer. He was, after all, breathing vile fumes on the man, hardly a shining example to a young law enforcement professional.

"Where is this Doa?"

"In the kitchen, Superintendent, with Mr. Pudkin and Mrs. Dempsey-Mohn."

The odors of cooking were pleasant but faint. "Doing what, please?"

"Deputy Minister Doa and Mr. Pudkin are playing chess, Superintendent. Mrs. Dempsey-Mohn is observing. I'm sorry, sir, but we've eaten every one of Mr. Pudkin's blintzes. They were extremely tasty."

"Splendid," Kiet said. "Please leave us alone for a while."

Kiet went into the kitchen. A chess game was indeed in progress. Susan stood, arms folded, viewing the combatants at the dining table. She smiled at Kiet and spoke a silent "hi."

Kiet played occasional and mediocre chess. His skills were instinctive and reactive, as if he were fencing. He lacked the dedication and intellectual discipline to challenge Luong's best. He qualified as a fan and for that reason was impressed, if skeptically, by Sergei Pudkin's reference to the renowned Boris Spassky.

Pudkin was in trouble, however. He muttered in Russian—his inflection universal, that of an obscenity—and castled. Kiet hadn't had time to analyze the layout, but most pieces were still on the board. He likened castling in this position to cranking up the drawbridge and praying that your provisions held out.

"Bobby Fischer, he do same to Boris in Reykjavik," Pudkin added.

His opponent stared at the board, too gentlemanly to suggest resignation. Pudkin's opponent, known to everyone in the villa as Deputy Minister of Defense Doa, had a smooth, amorphous face and wispy, black hair. Bright daylight revealed crow's-feet and sagging skin around the jaw, subtle hints that the man was in his early fifties. Kiet's cat was curled on his lap, purring loudly.

Pudkin studied his plight for several minutes, slid back his chair, and got up. "Okay, you win. I counter maybe, but I concede anyhow. Superintendent, you here, we must do the importants that supersede game. Minister Doa, he talk my asylum, but say he have to speak to you too."

"I'm afraid you've been misled," Kiet said. "Your chess adversary can arrange asylum to no farther than the Luongan countryside."

"Say what?"

The man scratched the cat's chin and said, "I apologize for the temporary deception. I had to see you, Bosha."

"Susan, Pudkin," Kiet said, sweeping his good arm, "may I introduce you to Ril Thoi, Chairman of the Central Committee of the Luongan Communist Party and undergraduate chess champion at Luong University a third of a century ago."

A moment of stunned silence followed. Susan recovered first. "To hell with a thesis," she said. "This is going to be a *book*."

Sergei Pudkin seemed starstruck by the presence of the Luong Rouge leader. Stammering made his accent nearly unintelligible. "Imperialist police chief and revolutionary hero, you friends? I no comprehend."

"Luongans cannot comprehend fellow Luongans," Kiet said. "Outsiders have no chance."

138

Could I have an interview, Chairman? Or is it General?" Susan asked.

"Comrade will suffice," Ril Thoi said, amused.

"And a photograph? I've never seen a picture of you."

Kiet answered for Thoi. "No. If he was recognizable, he couldn't be with us now. Your forgery of Cuong Van's handwriting was superb."

"He studied with us at the *lycée*, Bosha. I'd seen his papers."

"You always had an astounding memory, Ril."

"Every tiny talent must be utilized in the struggle," Thoi said.

"Ambassador Kalashnikov hate your guts, Comrade. He say you are stinking, revisionist Maoist and renegade to Marxist-Leninist precepts. True?"

Ril Thoi smiled benignly. "I am a Luongan fighting a people's war. Labels are meaningless and contradictory to the task."

Susan was by Kiet's side now, looking with concern at the patterned bruises on his forearm. Blood had scabbed in spots, points where Ref's fingernails penetrated. "What happened?"

"A wrestling match with snakes."

Kiet avoided her puzzled stare. Pudkin said, "My asylum, Comrade Thoi can no do, him being no Minister Doa. Kiet, what is status? Do you know?"

Kiet didn't know. He assumed Cuong Van was developing possibilities, but he didn't presently care now. His hangover was in bloom, Golden Tiger residues committing genocide to his brain cells. He wanted to scream, he wanted to sleep. Why was this eclectic bunch of troublemakers in his kitchen?

Kiet ignored Pudkin's question and took the chair he had vacated. "Ril, you've placed yourself in jeopardy to enjoy my hospitality. Tell me why."

"General Chi Vo," Ril Thoi said.

"If you resume where you ended last time, that nonsense about a younger militant faction of your Rouge, suicidal vengeance against Vo and Ref for the ambush, et cetera, I may be tempted to call my guards and have you arrested."

Ril Thoi stroked Kiet's cat's chin. The animal sighed in contentment, a sound Kiet had never been able to elicit. "I intend to be absolutely honest, Bosha. The youthful faction is reality. My hard-liners demand action and action requires resources. I compromised with them."

Kiet's thinking process fought through the Golden Tiger toxins. "Your compromise was to find a means of financing your war without figuratively spreading your legs for Soviets or Chinese or Vietnamese."

"You are too perceptive to be a capitalistic lackey, Bosha. Your talents are wasted serving an obsolete ruling class."

The rubies were in Kiet's left pants pocket. He managed to bend his aching body, dig them out with his right hand, and toss them on the table.

Ril Thoi's reaction to the rubies was flat and unsurprised. No wide-eyed gasp at their beauty and value, no attempt to fondle them. He surveyed the four stones as if counting beans and said, "Our socialist brothers in Burma came to us with an opportunity. The bribes and tariffs necessary to route them into Thailand were increasing."

"Ohhh! I see lesser color in rubies on scepter in Leningrad museum," said Pudkin, whose tone was neither flat nor unsurprised.

"Hush," Susan said.

"You took the rubies from the border to Obon," Kiet said. "That was your element. You turned them over to General Vo. He transported them to Hickorn. That was his element. He arranged to have them shipped to a buyer. You divided the profits. Dennis McCloud would fly them out of the country. Vo and his men shuttling between Hickorn and Bangkok would attract suspicion."

"The McCloud factor was speculation. Vo didn't confide details to me. But when McCloud was murdered, I *knew*."

"Knew what?" Susan asked.

"That somebody had betrayed somebody."

"I just want the bastard who killed Dennis to pay," she said. "I've lost my innocence about him, but nobody had any right to—"

She fled the room in tears. Kiet's instinct was to go to her, to hug her, patting her back, consoling. He didn't. His legs were leaden and Ril Thoi was talking in a straight line, factually, without a trace of dialectical materialism. Kiet *had* to hear the rest without interruption.

"How did you and General Vo make this marriage?"

"Authority he couldn't buy was weighing on his opium business. The Americans and their desire to defoliate poppies and to interdict smugglers with helicopters—it influenced a weak man who pined for his Hong Kong condominium. Pigeon blood rubies could bring more money faster to a decadent soldier eager to retire luxuriously. To me, they represented guns and bullets and supplies."

"Marsad Ref?" Kiet asked, flexing the fingers of his left hand.

"He wasn't a partner," Thoi said. "Not until the ambush. His ear was to the wall and he cut himself in."

Kiet pointed at the rubies. "Your nine men died for these?" Ril Thoi nodded.

"Future shipments?"

"None for now. Vo's agents will not communicate with mine. He sends patrols to the border, presumably to strike a bargain on his own with my Burmese comrades, but I've warned them off. The trade is postponed indefinitely."

"Vo fears retaliation for Ref's treachery, " Kiet said. "He knows you cannot trust him again."

"I could with stringent checks and balances, with Ref now in the capital, but I think Vo is too frightened. It's clear that Ref held more power than Vo in the Second District. Otherwise, Vo would have punished him for stealing the rubies."

"Your hothead faction, I presume they are more outraged over the loss of revenue to escalate your war than they are over the loss of their comrades in the ambush."

Ril Thoi shrugged. "Casualties are expected in a revolutionary struggle. There are less glorious ways to die than in combat with reactionary soldiers."

"Did you suspect all along that I had recovered your rubies?"

"Yes."

"If I gave you the rubies, your hotheads might settle down and you might have a tool with which to reestablish your smuggling business. General Vo would probably give you a larger percentage, all things considered."

"Quite probably, Bosha."

"And what am I to be given?"

"Marsad Ref," Thoi said. You can't prosecute him in your puppet courts, Bosha. He's too powerful. He'd have your witnesses killed."

"Your solution, please."

"Hickorn is decadent, but not hopelessly so. I have a cadre in the capital awaiting the time when they can throw off their chains."

"You'll kill him for me and justice will be done?"

"Yes."

Kiet groaned. "The vigilante justice of an insurgent. No!"

"Then your solution?"

142

"What is the cost of a consummated revolution, Ril? The price of a recoilless rifle? Supplies for the minimum of five thousand guerrillas you'd need to conquer the Royal Luongan Army, as pathetic as they perform?"

"The peasants—"

"The peasants, *hell*. They have enough rice to feed themselves and us too. They have no secret police terrorizing them in the night and telling them what to say and think. Your popular base, Ril, is a fallacy. The common man isn't going to throw down his hoe and pick up an AK-47 because you tell him to. If you want Luong, you'll have to take it by force, and several millions of black-market-ruby dollars won't buy you a week's occupation of Obon. Your ammunition would be expended and the Americans would nudge Royal troops in to overwhelm you. A bloody clash isn't your goal anyway. Tell me what these rubies really are about."

Pudkin broke in, "Kiet, you no have political consciousness. You blind to dissatisfaction of Luong citizens. Oppressed masses are poised to—"

"Shut your mouth," Kiet roared. "This isn't a stupid coffeehouse debate."

Pudkin flinched and began to rebut. Thoi shook his head. "Comrade, I appreciate your solidarity. Please go to the other room. Comfort the sad American lady."

Pudkin skulked out, mumbling in unintelligible Russian. Thoi said, "Bosha, Prince Pakse is old. He has no heirs. When he dies, there will be a vacuum."

"His Royal Highness is in splendid health."

"He is seventy-six years old. He'll live five years, maybe ten. General Vo desires retirement soon. Before and after he goes to Hong Kong, I'll have a solid infrastructure in the highlands."

"Vo the general as corporate executive, his troops employees in the ruby business. Opium too, when politics allows."

"We had such negotiations, Bosha. Ref and the rubies on your table are the stumbling blocks. A live-and-let-live attitude toward my people and me as long as profits roll in. Chi Vo dislikes problems."

"A coalition government, you ruling the highlands, a disorganized power play for Hickorn by His Royal Highness's successors?"

"It's a long-range scheme, Bosha. It'll satisfy my followers."

"Vo redefines corruption," Kiet said. "He'd sell Luong's northern provinces to you?"

"The price is attractive," Thoi said.

"How do you figure Marsad Ref?"

"I can't. That's my worry and Vo's. Ref's dream is power, not money. But to what extreme?"

"All right," Kiet said. "I'll work with you on the short haul to accomplish what I want to accomplish. Please take the largest ruby and sell it to Mr. Singh, proprietor of The Bombay Tailors. Use any identity other than your own."

"You have a plan, don't you, Bosha? Are you going to tell me what is is?"

Kiet rose and shook Ril Thoi's hand. "Of course not. We are enemies, you know. Haggle with the Indian, but not so much that he doesn't cheat you."

Ril Thoi said at the door, "If your plan succeeds, how will I know?"

"You'll know. You won't have to come here to ask."

Thoi smiled. "My hospitality is worn out, as they say?"

Kiet had been thinking: General Chi Vo sells the northern provinces, Ril is the purchaser. Who is more venal? One acts for business, the other for politics. In Luong, the words were too often synonymous.

"It is worn out," Kiet said honestly. "It is."

144

21

NEXT DAY, IN the morning, after Pudkin prepared a breakfast of kippers and a hash with ingredients that defied analysis but was nevertheless delicious, they came for him.

Deputy Foreign Minister in Charge of Eastern Affairs Mun Tai made the offer alone. His Mercedes sedan was parked outside and Kiet saw through his draperies that Cuong Van sat in the back seat. He understood the delicacy of the situation and forgave his old friend's snub.

Choices were restricted, Mun Tai explained. The circumstances of his defection were too cloudy, too potentially volatile to attract Western nations, but would Sergei Pudkin be amenable to a new life in Yugoslavia? There was a position for him in state-controlled electronics research and a man with his expertise would be embraced as a hero.

Yes, it seemed he would be amenable. Pudkin replied with a gleeful shout, clapping hands over his head as he performed a squatting, leg-kicking dance that startled the guards. Kiet recalled seeing similar folk-dancing in *National Geographic* by costumed Georgian peasants and was not startled at all. Susan beamed her approval by clapping along with him.

The humorless Mun Tai enjoyed the entertainment by staring at his watch, saying that a charter to Calcutta awaited at Hickorn International, asking if Pudkin could be ready in thirty minutes. Pudkin had no luggage, he was ready *now*. He hugged Kiet and kissed his cheeks, and gave Susan the same farewell, though hugging tighter, attempting a third kiss to the lips that she avoided.

When the Mercedes was out of sight, she asked Kiet, "Will you miss him?"

"No." A half truth. He had been looking forward to dinner.

"Yugoslavia is communist and it isn't. The best of both worlds for Sergei if he can't live in France."

"I know," Kiet said. "He can worship his ideology without the Red Army and the KGB endlessly critiquing his loyalty to communism. Belgrade and Sarajevo have neon, private automobiles, and plentiful markets."

"Are you saying he's a hypocrite?"

"I'm saying he is lucky. Will *you* miss him?"

"He was kind of fun, to a degree, like a cute puppy dog who has the revolting habit of doing you-know-what against your leg. No offense, but your quarters are cramped. We'd be bumping into each other and his hands would always be in the wrong places, accidentally on purpose, and he'd just happen to need to use the bathroom when I was already in there. Thank goodness the lock works."

Kiet suppressed his anger, the effort tongue-tying him. Jealousy? Ambassador Kalashnikov a voyeur, his scientific and engineering attaché a groper. He wondered if this peculiar Marxist lechery was a by-product of their dogma, indoctrination making covert sex normal.

"What are you doing today?" he finally said.

"The docks. Luong's fishing industry. Say, I've been meaning to ask. How come Ril Thoi calls you Bosha? The word isn't in my dictionary."

He heard a weak and strangled horn beep. Captain

146

Binh and his Renault Dauphine. Saved. "No comment," he said.

"Superintendent, you and Ril Thoi cooperating? I can't believe it. It blows my mind!"

Kiet was writing out a search warrant form as they drove to the Bombay Tailors. He looked at Binh, imagining his uniform cap exploding into threads from the hyperbole.

"It is an alliance of two confused men," he said. "Thoi's objective is rapprochement with General Vo. He thinks it will give him the highlands and the rubies. I'll grant him the latter. He can smuggle rubies until doomsday for all I care. If I have anything to say about it, his conquest of the highlands will have to be accomplished as it would be today, with rifles and mortars and heavy casualties. A satisfactory deterrent, as far as I am concerned."

"Rubies won't satisfy him."

"They'll have to. Marsad Ref is our common and most immediate obstacle. Thoi is assisting me for his reasons, me him for ours. Please drive faster."

Two patrol cars, manned by a pair of officers each, were parked across from the Bombay Tailors, per Kiet's orders. Kiet and Binh got out of theirs. Kiet waved them into position, the first set of troopers posted on the sidewalk in front, the second marching through the tailor shop, to seal the alley.

A pudgy Luongan in a sharkskin suit slowed his Peugeot, blinked at the activity, and pulled over a discreet three buildings away. Two elegant Caucasian women with sunglasses and long blonde hair—wives of French diplomats, perhaps—paused at the entrance to a store that sold overpriced lacquered furniture, delaying their shopping binge. A pack of Japanese tourists hesitated at their van and removed lens covers from their Nikons. Ordinary Luongans on the sidewalks, delivery people and store clerks, reduced their pace to slow motion.

"We have our audience, Superintendent," Binh said.

Kiet observed, amused that even the excesses of *Lé Avenue* could be boring if the alternative promised sufficient drama. Mr. A. Singh, proprietor of the Bombay Tailors, greeted them with a wide and joyless smile that suggested abscessed molars.

"Superintendent—"

Kiet cut him off by presenting the warrant.

"I don't—"

"We possess information that you're attempting to sell contraband, Mr. Singh, an item illegally imported to avoid duties."

"No, I—"

"Sir, you are being argumentative. Are you attempting to obstruct justice?"

"Oh, no, I—"

"Stand aside, Singh, and relax. If you are innocent, the worst you have to fear is my embarrassed apology."

Kiet and Binh brushed by him, made a cursory examination of the main shop, then went into the back.

"He probably has it on him," Binh said.

"Until the patrol cars appeared. I presume he was actively marketing the stone."

"Strip searches at the District of Columbia were quite fruitful when heroin and cocaine were involved."

"He knows that," Kiet said. "Start looking."

"There's a million shelves and drawers and boxes. He's a pack rat. Evidently he never discards anything." Binh whined, "I don't like the smell of this cubbyhole either. Singh burns incense."

"This will be easier than you think," Kiet said, digging through a bin of scrap cloth. "He had little time to transfer the ruby and he thinks we're stupid, a factor of his racial prejudice. These Subcontinent hustlers who play Hickorn's economy like a marionette, they believe we're addled *and* blind."

"Superintendent, how about this!"

Binh handed Kiet a bucket-sized wooden box of buttons, miscellaneous buttons of every size and shape.

Kiet's left arm felt today like it might not have to be amputated. He was able to hold the box without assistance from his other. "Our nominal tailor actually does sew and craft cloth. Remarkable. How many buttons would you say are in here?"

"Thousands," Binh said. "I'd guess at least half are rhinestones."

"Suitable for womens' attire."

Binh looked at him. "Singh doesn't handle ladies' fashions, just mens' suits when he isn't changing money."

"This stuff has accumulated over the years. As you stated, he refuses to discard." Kiet dumped the buttons on the floor and spread them with his palms into a single layer. The pigeon blood ruby twinkled in the midst of the junk, as if protesting the bad neighborhood. He began scooping everything back into the box.

"Aren't we going to confiscate it and arrest him, Superintendent?"

"No. Whether we find it or not, our mission is to authenticate rumors that the ruby is in circulation, in the marketplace."

They replaced the box, walked outside, and approached Singh. Kiet didn't notice an increase of spectators, but the crowd at the outset had remained, some blatantly eager for excitement, others lingering casually in the guise of minding their own affairs. The Japanese were snapping photographs.

"Well?" Singh asked.

"The Hickorn Police Department will be keeping an eye on you," Kiet said, shaking a finger.

"You didn't find your contraband, did you?" Singh said, a mocking confidence seeping into his smile. "You could have asked me what you were looking for. Instead, you treated me like a criminal."

"Behave yourself," Kiet said.

"Is that your apology?"

Kiet nodded to Binh and they walked to their car.

"I am an honest businessman," Singh shouted. "You and your incompetent storm troopers have dishonored me. You've damaged my business, Kiet. My customers will avoid me."

Just the opposite, Kiet thought: Nobody will henceforth doubt that you are a black-market czar. Binh tensed and Kiet tugged his arm. "Don't."

"Superintendent, we can't allow him to insult us in public."

"We can and will," Kiet said in a low voice. "I'm amazed at Singh's arrogance, but give him his glory. In the long run, the benefit is ours."

"Still, the loss of face—"

A comely young Luongan woman hurried over to Kiet. "Excuse me, Superintendent, is there a problem?"

The nametag on her blouse identified her as Lin Aidit, a Ministry of Tourism guide. She was with the Japanese. "Sorry, no real problem, but I can't comment further. Police business."

"I'm glad there isn't any trouble, Superintendent," she said. "My group has requested a favor."

"Of course. What?"

"Would you and the captain pose for a picture, please? They have complained that there isn't much to see or do in Hickorn."

"Superintendent!" Binh objected.

"Ah, our police raid is the high point of their day."

150

"They were terribly disappointed by the National Museum," Lin Aidit said. "These foreigners, they often bring unreasonable expectations to Luong."

"Come on, Binh, smile," Kiet said. "They'll go home to Japan with one dazzling memory. Other Japanese will visit. It's splendid for our economy. Miss Aidit, where did your contingent change their money, please?"

Her eyes widened. "I, I—"

"It's all right, I don't care. No harm."

"At the Bombay Tailors," she confessed. "Singh gives the best rate in town for yen."

"The superintendent of police confronting an arch-scoundrel. No wonder they are aroused. Let's do it."

Kiet stood close to Binh and grinned a Third World native's grin. Shutters clicked. They got into the Renault and left.

"Cheer up," Kiet said.

"How can I? Singh humiliated us, then that exhibition with the Japanese—it was mortifying."

"I regard the mission as highly successful."

"Successful? Tell me, Superintendent, am I missing something? In my view, we degraded ourselves and our case against Marsad Ref hasn't advanced an inch."

"It has, Captain," Kiet said. "Indirectly. The object of this exercise is Chi Vo."

"What will he do?"

"I don't know, but the knowledge that his ruby trade is out of his control may force him to do *something*. Your deft Siamese twin analogy? They have been separated too long to suit Vo. He's greedy. He'll believe Ref has the rubies and is selling them on his own."

"I see, Superintendent, but it's still too abstract for me to appreciate the value of what we subjected ourselves to."

"Abstract," Kiet said, liking the word. "It is indeed."

"Our next move?"

"Whoever we know in Obon, we'll call and ask them to watch Vo."

"Watch for what?"

"Anything, preferably panic."

22

"I KNEW LUONG didn't have radar. This really cries out the need for it, don't you think?" Susan said.

It was the following day, early afternoon. Kiet, Binh, and Susan were in the Citroën, heading from Kiet's villa to Hickorn International as quickly as possible. At dawn, an Obon police sergeant, a friend of Binh's who had been trained by Kiet, phoned Headquarters to report that a Lockheed Hercules marked SOUTHEAST ASIA AIR SERVICE had just landed.

The sergeant's home was directly under the airport's south approach and the aircraft shook his house, almost vibrating him out of bed if he was to be believed. Mammoth planes seldom visited Obon. Out of curiosity and anger for the lost sleep, he went to the airstrip, read the lettering on the fuselage of the four-engine turboprop, saw the august personage of Brigadier General Chi Vo greeting it, and notified Captain Binh.

Binh asked the sergeant to stand by at the airport and watch. Half an hour later, he had called Binh again, informing him that Vo and a variety of people and goods had been loaded, and that propellers were beginning to rotate, turbines whining to life.

Thus this necessarily wild ride that seemed to Kiet on the fringe of suicidal. Binh weaved through the pedestrians and bicycles and pedicabs and automobiles, the heel of one hand pressed on the horn button, narrowly avoiding mayhem to Hickornese, who had no concept of either urgency or orderly traffic.

"I can't conceive that a plane that big entered Luongan airspace and got all the way to Obon without being detected until Captain Binh's buddy called," she continued. "There must be *some* kind of air defense surveillance system."

Kiet had gone home for lunch to humor Susan, who had prepared mushroom quiche. His fork had just penetrated the fluffy yellow surface when Binh careened into his driveway. Susan hopped in with them, tagging along. There had been no time to protest.

A taxicab suddenly decided to make a U-turn in front of them. Binh slammed on the brakes, veered to the left, and scraped tires on the opposite curb. He swerved into the correct lane an instant before a collision with a bicyclist carrying a basket of papayas. Kiet blocked his eyes. If he was going to die like a kamikaze, best his trip to heavenly glory be a surprise.

"We have no air defense surveillance system because we have no air defense," he said, irritated at her naïveté. "We have no fighter planes. Bring in an armada of Chinese bombers and with the radar we don't have we cannot count the blips."

Kiet's logic seemed to daze her. She didn't reply. Binh said, "I checked with the Ministry of Defense about Southeast Asia Air Service, Superintendent. I spoke personally to Minister Van's aide-de-camp. It's a charter outfit registered in Hong Kong. The Hercules plane is a C-130 surplussed and sold to them by the U.S. Air Force."

"They flew non-stop from Hong Kong to Obon?"

"Presumably. As we know, they didn't clear Customs at Hickorn. It's a violation of law, but how do we enforce it?"

"By—how I hate saying this, I have no death wish—

getting to the airport before they're out of radio range. Drive faster, please."

Siesta time. Hickorn International Airport employees celebrated it with no greater or lesser enthusiasm than other Luongans. There was nobody around. It occurred to Kiet that the late Lon Min hadn't been replaced. So who was in charge, who would assist in preventing the escape of Chi Vo?

Binh ran to the offices and came back shrugging, answering his question.

"The control tower," Kiet said. "Surely somebody is on duty and the tower has a radio. Come."

They climbed spiral stairs of steel mesh. At the top, Kiet was taking air as if hoarding it. His calves and thighs felt like they had been whipped.

The lone occupant, the tower operator, hopped out of a swivel chair. He knew who Kiet was and came to a position of attention. A magazine he had been reading fell to the floor. Kiet picked it up. The paper was heavy and glossy. A triple-length page in the center hung out, a photograph of a young Caucasian woman splayed on beach sand. She was leering at the camera, licking her upper lip. She was naked and her legs were spread wide.

"Male chauvinism respects no borders," Susan said, looking away in disgust.

Binh confiscated the magazine and set it aside, slowly and intently, as if studying it for clues. "I've read this publication in America, Superintendent. The articles are intellectual and worthwhile."

"Yes, yes," Kiet said. He asked the tower operator, "Can you radio an airplane in the region, even if it is not en route to Hickorn?"

"Yes, on an open frequency," said the operator, who was edgy and eager to please. "What type of aircraft and where is it?"

155

"A Hercules, a private charter. It took off a while ago from Obon, bound for Hong Kong. I can't give you a location."

The operator looked at an aeronautical chart. "Unless it has permission to enter Chinese and Laotian and Vietnamese airspace, which isn't likely, it'll be forced to head south, passing near us toward Thailand, and swing northward over the South China Sea. The alternative is a SAM missile."

"Call them."

The operator did and a droning American voice crackled on the speaker. "Uh, Roger, Hickorn Tower. Go ahead. Over."

Kiet took the microphone. "What is your present position?"

No reply. The operator said, "Excuse me, Superintendent, but you have to say over."

"Over," Kiet snapped. "Where are you?"

"Uh, heading of one-seven-zero, first-leg-destination Bangkok Control, approximately fifty miles east of Hickorn. Altitude one-niner-thousand and climbing. Airspeed two-three-zero knots. What's the problem? Over."

"Change course immediately and land at Hickorn," Kiet ordered. "Over," he added, annoyed at the lingo.

"Uh, Hickorn Tower, request reason for deviation from flight plan, over."

"You're in violation of Customs laws. Foreign flights are required to clear Customs at Hickorn International Airport, in and out of country, over."

"Uh, Hickorn Tower, Customs procedure waived by Brigadier General Vo, our principal passenger."

"He hasn't the authority," Kiet interrupted. "Change course for Hickorn, over."

"Uh, Hickorn Tower, request denied. All Customs paperwork in order. Are currently three minutes from Thai border. Adios."

"God, he sounds just like Dennis," Susan said.

"Change course instantly," Kiet said. "This is official business. Failure to comply is violation of Luongan law."

Kiet listened to thirty seconds of static and said, "Failure to comply will result in a heat-seeking missile being fired up your tailpipe. Over, over."

"You don't have missiles and he probably knows it," Susan said.

Captain Binh smiled, immensely pleased by his superintendent's deception. "Agreed, he's probably ninety-nine percent sure. But if you're him, four miles in the air, would you take the chance?"

It seemed that the pilot would not. "Uh, Roger, Hickorn Tower. Am changing heading to two-six-five degrees. Request landing instructions, over."

Kiet handed the microphone to the sweaty-palmed tower operator, who jabbered aviationese into it.

"Well, what do we do with Vo when we have him on the ground?" Binh asked.

Kiet wished he had a definitive answer. An idea surfaced. "Your medical examiner, Dr. Pho. Bring him, please."

Binh's expression was a question mark.

"How long until they land?" Kiet asked the tower operator.

"Twenty minutes. I gave him a straight-in on Runway Two-Niner."

"Whatever," Kiet said. "Twenty minutes, Captain."

"Impossible, Superintendent."

"I have ridden with you, Captain."

Kiet ordered a taxi for the unwilling Susan. When the Hercules landed, shut down, and lowered its ramp, he walked up it alone. Two middle-aged Caucasian men wearing jumpsuits and caps cocked at jaunty angles met him, smoking cigarettes, sizing him up with the look that said, *this* is what bluffed us out of our jocks? Kiet sized *them* up as pilot and copilot, American expatriates chasing dollars, conveniently blind to their source. The aircraft struck him as a bloated version of Denny McCloud's Caribou, a ship showing its years and its justification for being retired by the U.S. military. Furniture and boxed belongings were lashed in the center, furnishings and—presumably—booty for Vo's Hong Kong condominium. People were strapped into their seats at the forward end, silent silhouettes in the darkness.

"This isn't gonna take all year, is it?" said one of the pilots. "This little shortcut's eating an extra thousand pounds of fuel and we're flying contract. We don't get to dip into any cost overruns."

Kiet recognized the voice. He was the captain, sans radio crackling. Kiet presented identification and said, "Not long."

"Tear this shit apart, you want. It's mostly junk, far as we can tell, clothes and stuff. Guy with his bucks—" the pilot cocked his head—"he could redecorate in Hong Kong, you'd think. Chief, that's what you are, Chief of Police, right? Chief, I swear if you're sniffing for opium, we don't know from opium. The general, he wrote the customs forms according to Hoyle. If he's got some opium stuffed up his bippy, he didn't clue us in. We're just taxi drivers, is all."

Kiet roamed his mind without success for a Customs officer named Hoyle. It didn't even have a Luongan ring. A jeep stopped at the foot of the ramp. Minister of Defense Cuong Van climbed out and joined him.

"Bosha, my aide relayed your Captain Binh's conversation with him. How were you able to bring Vo's plane in?"

158

"On wings of bullshit—" the pilot said, hesitating at the sight of Van.

Kiet couldn't take his eyes off Cuong Van either. The minister was dressed in his army uniform of starched khaki, gold general's lozenges on shoulder boards, and shoes polished like ebony mirrors. Cuong Van in uniform was an impressive visage.

"Psychology, Bosha," Cuong Van said. "Vo is a pitiful specimen of a commanding general, but he respects the image of rank."

Credibility, Kiet thought. Or was it stroking? One or the other of Binh's American designations for creative intimidation.

"Whatever's going on, gentlemen, we don't know anything about it," the pilot said in a more respectful tone. "But we'll bend over backwards to cooperate."

Van ignored the pilot and asked Kiet if he'd talked to Chi Vo yet. Kiet shook his head no. Van said to the Americans, "Go to your cockpit and latch the door."

And polish your dashboard, Kiet wanted to insert as the pilots obeyed without objection.

Kiet and Van went to where Chi Vo was seated. The pudgy general, never particularly soldierly even in uniform, gave the appearance of a bookkeeper awaiting a dentist's appointment, in dark business suit, white shirt, and regimental tie. His wife was at his side. Kiet recognized her from occasional visits to Hickorn. She was a drawn, graying woman who spoke when spoken to. On Vo's other side were two adolescent girls, their daughters. They were more attractive than genetics would dictate. Across the aisle was Vo's mistress. She was slightly older than Vo's daughters and possessed bulbous Caucasian breasts, Gaston LaCroix's soft globes.

"Chi," Cuong van said, "Retirement? Your papers haven't reached my desk."

"An oversight," Vo said.

"May we talk outside?" Van asked.

"If I leave the plane, will I be allowed to board again?"

Van looked at Kiet. Kiet said, "Absolutely. No charges will be filed, no unreasonable delays instituted."

The three men knew Kiet was lying. Chi Vo knew he had no choice. They exited into vivid blue sky and to the ninety-degree temperatures amplified to three digits by the asphalt tarmac. Vo began perspiring, wiping his forehead with a breast-pocket handkerchief not up to the task.

"I was perhaps in technical violation of our Customs laws, which are anyway subject to considerable abuse," Vo said. "That is inadequate reason to detain me."

"The law is the law," Kiet said, regretting the cliché before he was done speaking.

Vo ignored Kiet and said to Van, "I left an orderly chain-of-command. If I am politically persecuted, I cannot insure that those loyal to me would not retaliate."

"Vo," Cuong Van said, "you are an opium profiteer, a traitor who collaborates with the Rouge, and now you hint at anarchy."

Kiet had never seen Cuong Van so furious. Blood seemed to have drained from his face, and his body was a coiled spring. If he had been armed, Vo would be a dead man.

"Your words. Innuendos," Vo said, shaking his head. "But if you believe these lies, Mr. Minister, isn't Luong better served with me in Hong Kong?"

Kiet broke in, fearful that Cuong Van would commit murder with his hands and fists, "We're primarily concerned with the McCloud case."

"Kiet, are you stupid? I told you in Obon that I would help if I could, but I can't."

Just then, Binh's Citroën screeched to a halt beside them. Binh and Dr. Pho got out.

"It may be necessary to detain you after all, General.

160

For apolitical reasons," Kiet said. "Permit me to introduce you to Dr. Pho, Hickorn's chief medical examiner.
The post also charges him with some responsibility in
regard to the city's public health."

Cuong Van was the first to understand what Kiet was
doing. He uncoiled, folded his arms, and smiled broadly.

"My family and I are in perfect health, Kiet. What
kind of game is this?"

"Epidemics start with a single, relatively harmless
symptom, sir. No disrespect, but your eyes are rheumy.
Dr. Pho, could the General be suffering from beriberi?"

Dr. Pho was wary of the question, but nevertheless
anxious to cooperate with a man who had the power to
revoke his Hickorn Police Department contract. "Well,
possibly. Beriberi is a nutritional disorder that—"

"Then it isn't beriberi," Kiet diagnosed. "General
Vo's eyes are indicative of one carrying an infectious,
highly communicable disease."

"Typhoid?" Dr. Pho asked, a merchant displaying his
wares.

"Splendid," Kiet said. "Assuming this aircraft and its
occupants are infested with typhoid germs, how long a
quarantine would be required?"

"Quarantine?" said Chi Vo.

"Weeks," Dr. Pho said.

"Ridiculous, Kiet! We don't have typhoid."

"You do if Dr. Pho certifies that you do and seals the
plane and its occupants," Kiet said. "Think of it as an
opportunity for your wife and your concubine to become
better acquainted. Those American pilots, they'll also be
charming company."

"You can't—"

"We can," Cuong Van said, "As Superintendent Kiet
stated, medical quarantine is apolitical. Your stooges in
Obon won't know the truth. They'll pray for your recov-
ery."

161

Vo lowered his head in capitulation. "What is it you want, Kiet?"

"Information on Marsad Ref's role in Denny Mc-Cloud's death."

"He's guilty," Vo blurted. "He told me he killed him. McCloud crossed him and stole the rubies that rightfully belonged to me. Ref is a dangerous man. He betrays everyone. He laughed in my face. I . . . I was afraid of a confrontation. He had Lon Min killed too. He's a maniac with crazy friends. He would have killed me. If I sign a statement, will you release us?"

"Alas," Kiet said, "a statement isn't enough. You'll have to testify at his trial."

"We'll billet you and your family in the V.I.P. quarters at the Ministry," Cuong Van said cheerfully. "You'll be waited on in a style befitting a brigadier general."

"Guarded, you mean. Under house arrest."

"That is a pessimistic interpretation of my generosity," Van said. "A hero of the Kingdom, a soldier as distinguished as yourself, should not have to leave his luxurious quarters for any need, should he?"

The Hercules was unloaded, all contents and passengers trucked to the Ministry. The pilots demanded to know who was going to pay for the charter. Cuong Van sympathized and ordered them to be off the ground in thirty minutes. Van's driver returned Dr. Pho to his funeral parlor. Binh, Kiet, and Van took the Citroën into town.

"Ref's trial, Bosha," Van said. "You may be premature."

"Because General Vo's testimony will be hearsay and inadmissible?" Binh asked.

Kiet reminded him that the venue was Hickorn, not the District of Columbia. He said to Van, "Cuong, I don't like the sound of 'premature.' Vo was relayed the description of the man who sold Singh the ruby and

162

panicked as I had hoped. Nobody else recognized the seller as Ril Thoi, but Vo knew his partner too well. Vo realized his scheme was lost."

"He'll sing like a bird," Binh said. "A classic stool pigeon."

Kiet and Van puzzled at Binh's odd reference to edible fowl, then Van said, "Arrest of your suspect is the hitch, Bosha. I haven't seen Ref since the awards ceremony. He hasn't reported for duty. I was planning to break the news to you today."

"I'll put out an A.P.B. on him," Binh said.

"A what, please?"

"An all points bulletin," Binh said excitedly. "To every member of the Department. Utmost priority."

"No," Kiet said. "It's a waste of time."

Before Binh could argue, Van and Kiet groaned in unison, "The Soviet Embassy."

23

THE NEXT DAY had too few hours to suit Kiet, and too many. The street-renaming ceremony—Avenue Mao Tse-tung to Avenue Ronald Reagan—was set for noon. He didn't quarrel with the timing. The sun would be directly overhead and everyone and everything would sparkle, shadowless. Yet the affair would be finished, dignitaries and guests and workers safely indoors for air-conditioned cocktails and siestas, before the afternoon heat blistered and steamed the function into a cruel ordeal.

The hundreds of details required to provide security were accomplished, Kiet out of bed at an obscene six A.M. to begin attending to them. There was never enough time to be certain that all contingencies were anticipated, but when everything was done that could conceivably be done, Kiet could do nothing but wait and coax the clock to rush the formalities to an uneventful conclusion.

It was eleven-thirty and the nervous bustle of the morning had degenerated into an eternity of fidgeting. He had assigned five men to the site, to ring the podium at the intersection, and fifteen more at random positions in the swelling crowd. Three more were at the Hickorn Continental's rooftop, the command post he had decided to use. They were equipped with binoculars, rifles, and two-way radios. In a while he would join them, hovering nervously, suggesting this, ordering that, transferring his own anxieties to his officers.

For now he spared them and tried to relax on the *terrasse*. A Golden Tiger would be wonderful, but inappropriate. He hadn't eaten a bite today, but his knotted stomach surely would have rejected a plateful of fried Ma San shrimp. He sipped tea that was especially flavorless.

The two people he most had to protect were dictated by protocol to be the last arrivals. Ambassador Smithson. His Royal Highness. When they did show he would have even less appetite. His thoughts raced from crowd unruliness, those spontaneous outbreaks no one could predict, to possible trajectories from buildings. Luong's isolation had protected her from political assassinations, but Kiet was not comforted by travelogue serenity.

Until Susan sat down with him, he hadn't given a thought to the missing Colonel Ref. So fascinated was she by "a firsthand look at this esoteric political process" that he couldn't refuse her. Her Nikon and tape recorder hung around her neck like anchors. A harried guard stood behind her.

"Where have you been, please?" he asked.

"At ten, I told you I was going to mingle and take some notes and pictures. You said uh-huh. Remember?"

"I was preoccupied, but I didn't mean for you to wander about aimlessly," said Kiet, who hadn't remembered.

"Not aimlessly. *Au contraire*. The way people are jockeying for position on the street, it's like the Super Bowl." She put a hand on the uniformed sleeve of her guard. "He was with me. Acting like a father whose daughter blew curfew, okay?"

"You appeared from inside the hotel. Where else were you?"

"May I?" She poured tea from the pot into a cup. "As I said, I mingled. I came back here and went up to Dennis's room. I know, don't ask me to make any sense out of it either. I just wanted to see it, maybe walk in and take a last look around.''

"Did you?''

"No. It was locked. I saw the maid in the hall and she said the guest didn't want to be disturbed.''

Kiet spotted Gaston LaCroix coming out of the kitchen. As usual, the cadaverous hotel manager was dressed in Sydney Greenstreet whites. LaCroix saw Kiet too. Kiet excused himself and walked to him. He had an idea, a horrible idea, and wanted to pursue it privately.

"Superintendent, how nice—''

"LaCroix, you told me that Denny McCloud paid a month's rent in advance two days before his death.''

"Yes. Mr. McCloud always paid monthly.''

"McCloud was away from Hickorn frequently. Was his room used during his absences?''

"I don't understand, Superintendent. Our guests' rooms are regarded as their homes, whether they are in them or not.''

"LaCroix, did McCloud lend the room to his Luongan army cronies or to any other party when he was out of town?''

LaCroix frowned and scratched his chin, as if ransacking his memory. "Possibly. That is a prerogative of a paying guest.''

"Obon army officers who entertained young ladies?''

"Let me reiterate that I do not pry. Our reputation and the confidentialities enjoyed by my guests are interlinked.''

Kiet groaned. "Who is occupying the room today?''

"Over two weeks remain on his rent, Superintendent. While the man is dead, we respect rights of property, which his room privileges are, in essence. You are inquiring because of the estate? If by chance the room is being rented, a refund is in order, yes.''

166

Leave it to LaCroix to reduce any question to monetary terms, Kiet thought. "You don't know?"

"Well—"

Kiet took LaCroix's spindly arm. "Come. We'll go to the desk and look at your register."

"No, wait. It hasn't been rented. I'm fairly sure of that. I do vaguely recall a conversation with a friend of McCloud's who did point out to me that the rent was up-to-date and more. The friend was an intimate business associate of his, so I felt his continued use was appropriate."

"The intimate's name, please."

"Ah, let me think. The thousands of details inherent to this job, Superintendent. It's nigh impossible to remember everything."

LaCroix's face blanched the color of the bone stretched beneath it. Kiet had his answer. He looked at his watch: seven minutes until noon.

"LaCroix, refresh me. McCloud's room is on the top floor, is it not?"

"Yes. Room 406."

"On the north side."

"Northwest, one from the corner."

"Damn," Kiet said. "Give me your passkey and give it to me now!"

Kiet was beyond ordinary impatience and LaCroix knew it. LaCroix dug the keys out so fast that change came with them, tinkling on the tiles. Kiet grabbed the keys and ran toward the stairs. He saw Binh entering the *terrasse* and waved at him to follow.

Up they went, taking every other step. Kiet explained his idea en route.

"Superintendent, if it's true, you're unarmed. What did you expect to be able to do?"

A valid question, Kiet thought. "But you *are* armed. Your coming was my good fortune."

"We should have reinforcements."

"No time," Kiet said, gasping as they reached the fourth floor.

He paused a moment to gulp quantities of air into aching lungs. The disgustingly fit young captain waited for instructions, breathing normally. Kiet recovered sufficiently to start carefully toward 406, whispering to Binh that they would take opposite sides of the door. Binh would knock loudly while Kiet turned the passkey. The noise would muffle the door's unlatching.

"An excellent plan, Superintendent. Then what?"

Kiet shrugged. "We react."

They assumed their positions and Kiet touched the key to the lock. But instead of knocking, Binh pointed at the stairs. Kiet turned and saw Susan standing next to a maid's cart.

"Stay!" he hissed.

"Stay yourself," she hissed in return. "I'm not a dog."

Kiet tiptoed to her, summarized his theory, and glanced at his watch. "It's two minutes till. His Royal Highness will be coming by horse-drawn carriage. He is prompt."

"You really think Mars is in there?"

"We cannot take the risk that he isn't. Where is your guard?"

"Still downstairs, I guess. I told him I had to go potty. God, if Mars has any firepower at all, you guys are incredibly outgunned!"

"We have no time to arrange a favorable mismatch."

The maid belonging to the cart came out of a room. Kiet put a finger to his lips, gently herded her back in, and shut the door.

"This," Susan said, patting folded towels on the cart, "might be an ally."

Kiet looked at towels and sheets that were stacked on

a bottom shelf. There were more piled on top. A thick barrier of cotton and linen stretched from three or four inches above the floor to chest height. A bin of cleansers and disinfectants hung from a rail.

Kiet mouthed a silent thank you and rolled the cart to 406. Binh nodded, understanding. He drew his pistol. Kiet quietly inserted the key. Binh pounded as Kiet turned it.

No response.

Kiet twisted the knob, pushed the door in, and lurched backward. Simultaneously, Binh shoved in the cart with an extended leg.

The cart began to rock. The material on it seemed to undulate. Chunks exploded from the sides and top, small white eruptions. Negligible sound, five seconds of staccato puffs. A silencer, Kiet knew.

"He's reloading," Binh screamed, rushing in and firing blindly.

Kiet entered behind him, in a crouch. A man wearing the scruffy fatigues of a Rouge guerrilla was trying to insert a fresh clip into an assault rifle. Binh had expended his magazine too, missing, and went after him, holding his pistol by the barrel. The man ducked a roundhouse swing. His foot shot out, knocking the pistol from Binh's hand.

Kiet dove for the guerrilla, jarring him before the replacement clip locked, but the man, though small, was immensely strong. He shook Kiet loose with a clublike elbow to the ribs. Binh swung a fist, but the man's quick reaction denied him solid contact. He countered with a blow to Binh's jaw that sent him to his knees, his eyes rolling.

Kiet hugged the guerrilla and rode him to the floor. Thick black hair under his cap. A bandit moustache. Fearsome eyes. These images recorded as Kiet, clinging desperately, crabbed along the rug, nearer and nearer to the rifle. Just as Marsad Ref grasped it and tucked his knees under Kiet's belly, ready to eject his burden, a flurry of sobbing and screaming and flailing arms caused Ref to release his grip on the weapon.

Susan was kneeling, swinging a metallic cylinder, striking Ref's face over and over, initial wildness given way to the rhythmic efficiency of a woodchopper. The black wig and cap immediately gone. Pasted-on moustache removed in chunks. Nose cracking like a chicken bone. Blood droplets splashing Kiet like a windblown monsoon shower.

Marsad Ref went limp under him. Kiet rose and fell forward, toppling Susan and himself.

"Stop. Stop. It's done, it's finished."

They clung, her sobbing, his eyes watery, face-losing sounds of weakness and emotion suppressed with a will he didn't think he possessed.

There were five people in Room 406, the four principals of the fight and Gaston LaCroix. Susan was composed, sitting on the edge of the bed, saying that for the first time since she had licked the habit two years earlier she was dying for a cigarette. Captain Binh's mouth was swollen and Kiet could not convince him to visit a hospital. If his jaw was broken, medical attention would have to defer to priorities.

In Binh's hand was an assemblage of bent wire and crushed porcelain, a molar bridge provided in America by his District of Columbia hosts and their excellent dental insurance plan. The Hickorn Police Department had no such benefits and the imminent expense seemed to depress Binh. Kiet made no promises, but vowed to himself to get Binh's dentistry repairs paid for by the Department, whether creative accounting was required or not.

Colonel Marsad Ref was resting uncomfortably on

406's carpeting, in a semi-fetal position, appendages secured and joined with an entire fifty-yard roll of strapping tape. Kiet imagined a mummy, a pharaoh with enemies who had interred him hastily and contemptuously.

Ref was awake, his lumps and scabs superficial, but he stared at an unknown point on a nonexistent horizon, communicative as any Egyptian who had lain shriveled in a box for five thousand years.

LaCroix scrounged the tape for Kiet. He had burst in, bearing guest complaints about the noise, surveyed the chaos, closed the door after him, volunteered complete cooperation, and sat. Kiet had mused that even a magpie knew when to perch in silence.

The superintendent was pacing slowly, thinking, working on an assemblage of his own—organization of facts and speculation on what was intended, what had been prevented.

Facts: Ref's rifle, silencer, and sniperscope were of Chinese manufacture. The windows in 406 were opened wide. The presumed targets, His Royal Highness and Ambassador Smithson, would have been easy victims, helpless as targets on a shooting range. Ref wore his army uniform under the guerrilla garb.

Speculation: A peeling of outer clothing and a quick escape for Ref. Ten to fifteen seconds consumed by the killings. Ample time for a score of witnesses in the crowd of hundreds to see the shaggy communist assassin. Thanks to the silencer, insufficient time for security officers to react and answer the fire. Weapon left in room, evidence damning the monstrous Ril Thoi and his Chinese conspirators. Rouge fatigues discarded elsewhere.

Motivation? Only his homicidal mummy could elucidate and Kiet wasn't hopeful. He said to Binh, "The ceremony ended half an hour ago. One of us should report to our men and release them to normal duty. Are you up to it?"

Binh nodded yes, but said, "Ikinsupintentifay."

"I applaud your dedication, Captain. No. I'll go. In my absence, nobody is to leave this room. Except you, LaCroix. Tell me, do you have a larger custodial cart?"

"Yes, Superintendent. A big canvas one for dirty linen when an unusual number of guests check out on a particular day."

"Could it conceal a man?"

"Yes."

"While I'm away, please bring it to this room."

Binh asked, "AllntweallestRef?"

"Arrest him?"

Binh nodded eagerly. Kiet felt compassion for Binh's pain and his speech impediment, but the blacker side of him gave thanks that there would be no recitation of Miranda warnings. "This is an unusual circumstance. Colonel Ref must participate in that decision."

Marsad Ref spat a gob of phlegm and blood, aiming at Kiet but missing.

"My baser instincts are rooting for you to feed him to the Ma San River fish," Susan said.

Kiet waited for a disclaimer, a clue from her eyes or lips that would say it was just a remark made in cynical jest. No.

"This man in the cart, he will be heavy, and the Continental lacks elevators," LaCroix said.

"Not a word to your employees," Kiet said. "We'll manage ourselves."

"Bluuvwat?"

"At nightfall," Kiet said, delighted that he was learning this new language. As he went to the door, he stubbed a toe on the metal cylinder that had subdued Ref. He was annoyed that he hadn't thought to examine it earlier. This was an omission of primary police procedure.

172

He hefted it, a kilo or two of pressurized liquid. Evidentally Susan had taken it from the maid's cart. The label identified it as a disinfectant that killed germs, mold, and mildew, and eliminated odors. The script was in English, but the brand name looked French. Lysol. The cylinder was rippled with shallow dents.

Susan reached out for it. "In case Mars needs his mouth washed out while you're gone."

Binh and Kiet trundled the canvas-sided cart down four flights of steps to the Continental's delivery bay. In darkness, they lifted Ref into the Citroën's trunk and slammed the lid. Before the transfer they had remummified him. Binh pressed his pistol to Ref's ear as Kiet removed the Rouge fatigues. More tape was then applied. Colonel Marsad Ref was now wearing Royal Luongan Army khaki, although Kiet doubted that the senior officer and his finery, gold-braided cap and all, could pass a parade inspection.

Kiet told Binh where to drive. Binh asked, "TaintellogfustbefoHaquaters?"

"Yes," Kiet said.

They parked and Kiet unlocked the trunk, raising it enough so he could talk to Ref, but not enough for his prisoner to see much.

"Ref, this is your best opportunity to speak to me. You believe you're impervious. Your present relationship with a spare tire is proof you're not."

Ref spoke, startling Kiet. He hadn't expected a reply so early in the interview. "Where are we, at your jail?"

"No."

"Good for you we're not, you overstuffed piece of shit. If I'm arrested, you won't live the night. The Second District is mine, you know. Chi Vo, that pig, he danced on the end of my strings. I have friends."

"The same friends you paid to kill Lon Min?"

"They'd put your fat body in a grave as a favor to me."

"Who are your accomplices in the assassination scheme? And why, you bastard, would you wish to kill His Royal Highness?"

Ref did not respond.

"Answer my question, please."

"Are you going to charge me and try me in a court? Kiet, you're fat *and* stupid."

"You're intimating that we'd never meet at a trial?"

"If your life is important to you, Kiet, turn me loose now. We can become friends. You're a valuable man. I could use you as an ally."

"Allied in what, please?"

"Behave and do what I tell you to and you can be a rich, powerful man."

"A most attractive bribe offer. Elaborate, please."

"Get this fucking tape off me, Kiet, and do it now. I'm losing patience."

"Very well," Kiet said. He lifted the trunk lid and freed Marsad Ref's arms and legs with scissors.

Ref staggered out and rubbed his wrists. He looked around and saw that they were on a wharf next to the Foh Ten Bridge. He also saw Binh's pistol pointed at his face.

"Ref," Kiet said, "you're correct that a trial without your cooperation would be disastrous. Innocent Luongans would die from the turmoil you'd cause. I don't question that you are capable of instigating a civil war."

"We have an arrangement?"

"I may consider a guilty plea. I despise the very notion of it, but an arrangement, as you say, would require a contrite and detailed confession by you. Your reward would be exile. You would receive a conditional death sentence that would be carried out if you ever returned to the Kingdom of Luong."

174

"Fuck you, Kiet. Order your idiot assistant to lower his gun and allow me to—"

Binh cocked the hammer and took a step closer.

"Stupid," Ref said.

"*This* is stupid, Colonel," Kiet said, showing Ref the rubies. "Your obvious aim is to own Luong, yet you kill for a few stones. Why?"

"I was cheated, Kiet. You're an honorable man. You would do the same."

Kiet would not, but he understood Ref's psychopathic code. Take something from me and I will kill you. Denny McCloud had known too, but daring without efficiency had failed him.

"You are free," Kiet said. "Free to walk across the bridge. Foh Ten is your exile."

"No!"

"That car across from us. Two of my most discreet officers. They and their relief shifts have orders to shoot you on sight if you try to cross back into Hickorn. You have friends in Foh Ten who killed Lon Min for you, but I doubt if they are real friends, especially since you're being sent in without money. Your tenure at the Royal Military Academy, your brutality, the deserters in Foh Ten, not to mention generic thugs crouched behind every shanty. How long do you think you would survive?"

"Kiet, you're reputed to be civilized. You wouldn't do this."

"I don't want to, but the alternative is your chaos. Agree to my conditions and we'll drive to Headquarters."

"I'll be seeing you again, Kiet," Ref said, walking to the bridge.

Binh and Kiet watched as he walked halfway across, raised a fist, then vanished into the night.

"Dayathunhemakit?"

"Will he make it, will he survive? Ref has enemies

lurking throughout Foh Ten, but he is meaner than most of them. Perhaps.''

"Heedekcapjustis."

Kiet put his arm around Binh and led him to the car. "He might or might not escape justice in a courtroom too. I think the probabilities are similar and this informal method keeps politics at bay. Come. I know a dentist who will work late if we talk sweetly to him."

24

"I COMPLIMENT YOU, Superintendent. Your investigation was resourceful and courageous," said Prince Novisad Pakse as he placed his cue ball on the billiards table.

Kiet stood off to a side, as stiffly as his soft girth would permit. Susan Dempsey-Mohn was with him in the Royal Palace billiards room. Both were summoned guests.

"Thank you, Your Highness," Kiet said.

Prince Pakse studied the triangular rack of balls on a table whose dimensions exceeded several rooms in Kiet's villa, then shot the cue ball with a long thrust of his stick. Colored balls exploded every which way. His Royal Highness was tiny and elderly, and the clattering force of the impact surprised Kiet. The prince was dressed in a black tuxedo, which Kiet knew to be the standard tournament uniform of what were known as "hustlers" and "pool barracudas." His Royal Highness found the clothing strange and uncomfortable, but also wore it during practice to better acclimate himself for competition.

Prince Pakse applied blue chalk to the tip of his stick and said, "Is it your impression, Superintendent, that Colonel Ref's assassination attempt was premeditated far in advance?"

"No, Your Highness. I believe it was expediency created by his unexpected transfer to Hickorn and progress made in the McCloud murder."

"Do you feel that he was willing to bide his time at Obon until this chain of events?"

"Yes, Your Highness, I do. He had subverted General Vo's authority at Second District and, through the ambush, separated the business partnership between Vo and the Rouge. If the unthinkable happened, he would be poised to lead a coup d'etat against weak and disorganized Hickorn factions."

Prince Pakse shook his head sadly and dispatched the three-ball into a side pocket. The cue ball spun in reverse, as if on a string, and came to rest in the center of the table. "I think at times I am cursed, Superintendent. I have no direct heirs, no sons and daughters or living brothers and sisters to succeed me, but my extended family of first and second cousins and the products of their marital unions hover above my head as though I were tomorrow's carrion. Lon Min, for instance, whom I do not mourn. When I die, I do not envy those like yourself loyal to the Kingdom and its stability, and the power struggle you will have to endure."

"A dead American writer of repute said that reports of his death were exaggerated, Your Highness."

"Alas, I am not a young man." The seven-ball disappeared into a corner pocket. "My demise yesterday was barely avoided, thanks to you and the young and ravishing Caucasian lady. I am convening Parliament next week, Superintendent, to add to our Constitution a specific and unbreakable clause for succession. Ambassador Smithson, that pompous bore, he nags me incessantly to amend our Constitution to resemble the American model. Perhaps he is shrewder than I have given him credit for. What is your theory on Soviet involvement in this debacle?"

"You said farewell to Ambassador Kalashnikov at the airport this morning, Your Highness. An unexpected farewell."

178

The nine-ball followed the seven-ball. "His beloved nephew in Novomoskovsk is ill with a persistent infection. He departed on an extended furlough."

Susan snickered.

Prince Pakse looked at her and smiled. "A Marxist lecher, a grim stolid exporter of revolution clutching binoculars with sweating palms. That is an amusing image, but I cannot blame him. Apparently his infatuation with one so near another who was interlocked in the skulduggery was a coincidence. Hickorn is not a huge city. Coincidences are common, but this one was extremely fortuitous."

Susan's snicker degraded into a blush.

"You have requested an interview with me for your scholarly paper, Susan? You shall have it when Superintendent Kiet and I have completed our seamy business."

"Thank you, Your Highness."

Kiet said, "In answer to your question, Kalashnikov and the Russians had washed their hands of the Rouge eons ago. Ril Thoi is the brother of my pet cat. He behaves as he chooses and if you tried to fit him with a leash and a collar, your hands would become scratched and bloody. Kalashnikov sees Ref, I think, as the counterpart of the Cuban, Fidel Castro. He would expect him to take over Luong with brutal persistence. Then, like Castro, he would be absorbed into the Russian camp when he came to realize, as he inevitably would, that communist socialism was the path toward which Luong should steer.

"You, Your Highness, would be martyred by Ref's people, and revered by the regime as a horrifying object lesson to those who subscribed to the promises of Ril Thoi and his nonexistent Chinese allies."

Prince Pakse paused. The ball he desired to strike was blocked by another. "Superintendent, my seventy-six years of life on this planet have been gladdened by unending luxury. I want for nothing. Perhaps that is why I cannot understand Ref's obsession with four precious red stones. It seems illogical to one to whom riches have always been available."

"It *was* illogical, Your Highness. But I think that Ref's concern was not so much for the stones as at being cheated, and insisting on the ultimate vengeance. Dennis McCloud had smuggled opium for Vo, and then the more fascinating rubies. Ref thought he could do some smuggling of rubies of his own, bypassing Vo. He gave McCloud the stones and requested that he carry them out. But McCloud didn't trust Ref, who after all, had betrayed Vo, and the rubies were a temptation. They became McCloud's permanent ticket out of Luong. Ref rode on McCloud's last flight, perhaps to attend to other business in Hickorn, perhaps not. In any case, he became suspicious and demanded to see the rubies just prior to McCloud's departure to Bangkok. And McCloud could not produce them."

"Why not, Superintendent?"

Kiet hesitated.

"It's okay," Susan said. "As you've said a million times, Hickorn is a town of gossip and rumors. I know that Dennis swallowed the damn things."

"I can guess why McCloud swallowed them," Kiet continued. "He was headed nonstop to Australia, where customs procedures are quite strict. He had installed auxiliary fuel tanks in his Caribou weeks before, anticipating, I think, a confrontation between Ref and Vo, and such an opportunity."

"I cannot argue with your conclusions."

"Have you decided what is to be done with General Vo, your Highness?"

"Minister Van and I have discussed the matter at length. General Tranh, present commander of the Royal

Military Academy, is retiring. We are promoting Vo to major general and giving him that job.''

Prince Pakse banked the cue ball off a cushion. It returned to the hidden ball from a different angle and grazed it. The ball rolled into a side pocket.

"Nice shot," Susan said.

"Ah," Kiet said. "Academy commanders traditionally arise with the students and cadre and join in the morning calisthenics.''

"The tradition will continue," Prince Pakse said. "Vo is flabby and dissipated. The austere regimen will be highly beneficial to his health, much more so than soft retirement in a Hong Kong condominium.''

"I agree," Kiet said.

"Bosha, I must ask you, have you any qualms about the manner in which you dispensed justice to Marsad Ref? You acted outside our justice system, you know.''

"I do, Your Highness, but it was an exceptional situation.''

"It was indeed. I share your trepidation about bringing Ref to trial. He has the destructive proclivities of a mongoose.''

"Bosha?" Susan said. "Will somebody please tell me what it means?''

Kiet groaned.

"I apologize if the use of your nickname seems overly familiar, Superintendent," Prince Pakse said.

"No apologies necessary," said Kiet, who was at once embarrassed and flattered.

"Well?" Susan asked.

"It is slang in Luongan for runt," Prince Pakse explained. "His *lycée* classmates pinned it on him. This giant you see did not spurt in growth until late adolescence.''

Kiet remembered how his arms and legs ached when he grew twelve inches in two years.

"Bosha," Susan said, beaming.

"No comment," Kiet said.